The Warrior of the Glen

~~ The Glen Highland Romance ~~

Book 6

Michelle Deerwester-Dalrymple

The Warrior of the Glen

Table of Contents

If you love this book, be sure to leave a review! Reviews are life blood for authors, and I appreciate every review I receive!

Want more from Michelle? Click below to receive Gavin, the free Glen Highland Romance short ebook, free books, updates, and more in your inbox

Get your free copy by signing up here!

Chapter One: The Inn

Invercassely, Northern Highlands, 1307

THE INN AT CHISHOLM welcomed Rafe with a scent of ale and piss. The inn was crowded and the fire weak, but 'twas a welcome change to the steady drizzle that had plagued him as he made his way south toward the Great Glen.

Few heads turned his direction at the door banging open against the wind, as most had more concern for their drink than strangers entering the tavern.

Jingling his coin in his sporran, Rafe considered how much mead and meat he might buy and still have enough for a room. He didn't relish sleeping outside in the rain if he could avoid it.

After leaving his clan lands, Rafe had headed south, rounding Loch Fannich, and the weather remained a steady drizzle. Not a torrential downpour, but just enough to keep him uncomfortably damp. The hospitality of locals kept a thatched roof over his head for the past few days. However, this deep in the Fraser lands, caution required him to keep his distance.

As 'twere, he'd already told enough tall tales to ensure his next confession with the priest to be a long one.

The Frasers had a lengthy history of feuding with the MacKays, a violent feud at that. Men had died in those conflicts, many of them Frasers, and while Rafe had not participated, being either too young or not invited, he still carried the weight of that bloody conflict on his shoulders and in his name.

He didn't ken why the protracted feud existed — old folk tales shared a myriad of possibilities: a scorned woman, a murdered son, betrayal to a king long gone. All he knew was it was fortunate for him that a breadth of clan lands separated his from the Frasers. Now that Rafe was here with the Frasers, he needed to keep his false history consistent.

As he journeyed south, he let the lies form, trying to logic out the more believable falsities. The first thing he needed was a new name. Rafe, he could keep. His first name had sufficed thus far. A fair number of Highlanders were named for Archangels. But MacKay, 'twas hated throughout the lands.

MacLeod, conversely, was a small clan in the western Highlands with little troubled history.

'Twould be a perfect name to replace his own. Rafe MacLeod. Now he must remember to answer to it.

"Do ye want a drink? Or are ye going to stand there like a fool?" A voice from his left pestered, and Rafe turned his pale blue eyes to the barkeep who had called out to him. "Either ye pay for something or ye leave. The fire's nay free, ye ken?"

Still dripping, Rafe pushed past several men standing at the counter to order a warm mead and inquire about a meal and a room. The cost was thankfully less than he'd anticipated, and he requested both.

A slender, doe-eyed barmaid appeared from behind the bar and led him to his narrow room at the end of the hall so he could peel off his plaid and leave his belongings. The room was low-roofed but dry, which was most important for Rafe as he listened to the rain whip up its intensity outside. Grateful for any roof over his head, he sat on the saggy hay bedding and awaited his meal.

After his meager meal of stringy boiled beef and dry bread, he laid on the bed, his arms crossed under his head, and stared at the warped beams of the roof. Time to contemplate his situation.

Rafe really didn't know where to go from here. He'd heard the Bruce was south, but that could be anywhere from the Lowlands to the Great Glen. He wanted to keep his ears open, mayhap ask some questions to learn where the Scots army camped. Mayhap the barkeep knew? Rafe's prospects at finding the Bruce were dismal at best.

A rousing cheer erupted from the barroom downstairs. Rafe tipped his head toward the door. Any inquiries about joining the

Bruce would have to wait until the next day. The crowd was too drunk to recall their own names, let alone the location of the Bruce, to bother asking this eve. Rafe would have preferred to join them in their libations, but the coin in his sporran dictated otherwise, especially if the rain didn't abate and he was forced to remain at the inn another night.

A flash of light reflected in his room, followed by an earth-shattering crack of thunder. Aye, 'twas an excellent chance he may need to hole up until this storm passed. Resigning himself to an early bedtime, he yanked off his muddy boots and tossed them near the door.

Pulling his mangy tunic over his shoulders, Rafe hung it on the peg of the headboard. Just as he settled onto the tartan coverlet, a light tap sounded at his door — so light he wasn't sure he heard anything. He pressed his ear to the door. Perchance the knock came from farther down the hall?

The hesitant knock sounded again, definitely on his door, and Rafe yanked it open. The slender barmaid stood before him, wearing only a middy shift and her plaid *arasaid*. Her doe-eyes squinted slightly as the corner of her mouth curled in invitation.

"Mayhap the man might want company this eve?"

She needn't have asked — her smile and state of undress told him why she was at his chamber door. And a sober lone man was more of a welcome customer for a whore in a bar than a drunk with inebriated friends. Rafe's mind thought of what little coin filled his sporran.

"How much?" he asked. Though he was searching for more in this life — 'twas the whole reason he left the MacKays — soul searching was a lonely occupation. If the price was right, company was most welcome.

"I'll take a silver penny if I can stay wi' ye for the night."

I'll have to hide my sporran. The lass could well be a whore and a thief.

"One moment, lass," he told her before closing the door. After he extracted a single coin, he stuck his sporran in the hay bedding, nestling it deeply. Then he opened the door wide.

"I welcome your company," he said, handing over the penny.

Her wide eyes lit and that curl of a smile grew.

"As I welcome yours, milord," the lass said in a coy voice, stepping inside the room.

Rafe did not retire early that night. Fortunately, the noise of the storm covered the passionate storm of their exertions. The lass was a loud and eager lover.

And when they did eventually find their slumber, Rafe wrapped his arm around the slim lassie, curling into her. They slept hard, not once awakened by the ferocity of the weather outside or the raucous men below.

The lass was gone when he finally woke the following morn. His plaid, boots, and hidden sporran remained.

Rafe smiled to himself. An honest prostitute was a rare thing indeed.

***

The rain, if possible, grew worse over the course of the morn. The deluge kept most of the inn's patrons inside, close to the fire, and the inn served as a refuge for those unfortunate souls traveling. The main tavern room was cramped beyond capacity, something which undoubtedly pleased the innkeeper to no end.

Rafe kept to himself, nursing a mug of honeyed mead in the dim corner of the room. He used the time to watch those celebrating the day or eating dry food for the first time in days. 'Twas not what he had planned for his journey to find the Bruce's army, but getting waylaid at an inn during a storm was not the worst way to occupy one's time.

Just after the noontide meal had been consumed by bored patrons, a small party of men pushed into the already crowded room, taking up space at the bar counter. Dripping muddy water on the warped floorboards, the party of men had obviously spent a good deal of time on the road.

The newcomers interested Rafe, who kept an eye on them as they found a warm reception at the bar, mostly because the largest of the men held a heavy sporran aloft, filled with coin he was ready to spend on food and drink and rooms. Their dull tartans dropped to their seats as they warmed, and their conversation grew louder as they drank.

Rafe heard one man say "Fraser," and his ears perked. Stories of the MacKay blood feuds with the Frasers were common stories — one such feud was so dark. From the rumors Rafe could recall, it had ended badly with the death of several of the Fraser men. 'Twas said that the Laird never forgave the MacKays and swore vengeance against them if he ever came across their sort anywhere in the Highlands. Rafe sunk down in his chair, as though these men might know Rafe's connection to the MacKays.

He'd also heard their clan were staunch Bruce supporters. Perchance he could hear more of the Bruce's movements, gain a better idea of where to locate the Scots army, and work his way there. Shifting his broad shoulders, he leaned toward the Frasers, trying to overhear. However, the more the crowd in the packed room drank, the louder they became, and Rafe lost the Fraser conversation in the din.

His deep blue eyes scanned the room by the bar counter, looking for a closer space for eavesdropping. Rising from the uncomfortable seat in the corner, Rafe moved through the gauntlet of the tavern, searching for a chair, a stool, or even an empty spot near the counter.

Just as Rafe shifted past a portly fellow who was spilling his ale down the front of his tunic, he accidentally slammed into a shorter man hidden behind the fat fellow's girth.

The young man appeared to be a youth and couldn't have weighed more than six stone. The lad launched backward, landing at the feet of his kinsmen. Immediately contrite, Rafe reached a hand down to help the lad back to his feet. But before he could grip the lad's arm, three barrel-chested men surrounded Rafe, a protective wall blocking his view of the younger man. Rafe was of a good size, a sound warrior, but these men . . . they were titans.

"What's wrong with ye, ye feckin fool? Are ye no' watching where ye are going?"

Rafe tried to step back from the giant's intimidating scrutiny.

"Nay, I—" Rafe stuttered, bumping into the solid mass of the other Fraser man standing behind him. *Oh no.* This was *not* the introduction he wanted with these men.

"Why don't ye pick on someone more your size?" the second Fraser asked.

By this time, the lad had managed to pull himself up to his full, short height, straighten his bonnet atop his mess of bronze hair, and insert himself between the mountain of a man and Rafe.

"Christ's blood, Nevan! Leave off the poor man! Can ye nay see ye've put the fear o' the de'il in him?" he commanded in a pitched voice.

The men continued to glower, but the youth (*the heavily protected youth,* Rafe thought. *He must be important, the son of a chieftain mayhap?*) smiled widely and offered his arm in welcome. Rafe clasped it in return.

"Never ye mind these lug-abouts. They just like to play the ogre. They are truly baby cats if ye ken them well."

The lad was even younger and more clean shaven than Rafe initially realized, the smudge of dirt on the lad's jaw notwithstanding. The smudge appeared to be intentional, to make it appear that the lad had more facial hair than was present on his face. The young man dropped his hand and waved Rafe toward the counter.

"I'm Bren. Bren of clan Fraser. These here are Nevan, Duncan, and Kellan, brothers all. Cousins to me. Will ye share a drink with us, uh . . ." The lad's words trailed off, and it dawned on Rafe that he was looking for an introduction.

"Oh! Aye! Name's Rafael. Rafe. Rafe MacK—" He stopped speaking abruptly. He'd already forgotten he could not well introduce himself under his true name! This clan was in a blood feud with the MacKays. That one word would have been a horrible misstep. These giants surely would have pounded him into the floor if he'd finished saying his name.

"Mac?" It seemed to Rafe the four men waited with edgy breath for him to finish his name. Rafe struggled until the lie he'd planned earlier came to mind.

"Leod. Rafe MacLeod."

"Ooch, of Clan MacLeod to the west?" one of the men asked. Rafe swallowed hard, taking his time to answer.

"Aye, but I've been away with my distant kin. Now I'm headed south to join with the Bruce."

The crowd near them erupted in a chorus. "The Bruce!" they cheered before gulping their drinks and slamming their tankards on the counter. Rafe jumped at their interjection.

"In this weather? Ye have a far distance to go," Bren confirmed Rafe's suspicions. "I've heard he's most likely near Dumfries, planning his next strategy against the English. But he may no' remain there long."

The lad slid a mug of ale at Rafe, encouraging him to drink. Rafe took a swig, trying to formulate his lies to align as close to the truth as possible. Rafe didn't have much of a lying tongue. And less of a sound memory when drunk.

"I've heard the same. I hope to join him afore he moves on."

"Did ye plan on traveling in the storm?" Bren asked.

Rafe finally allowed himself a relaxed smile.

"I did no' anticipate such rain when I set out. It has slowed my progress, truly."

The lad laughed and clapped Rafe on the back. 'Twas lighter than a bird's wing, so frail was the lad's touch. *A sickly lad? Younger than he appeared?* Rafe wondered. Something was not quite right with the laddie. 'Twould explain the cousins' overly protective nature toward the youth.

The afternoon passed quickly as the four men sat with Rafe, sharing tales of Fraser clan pride and youthful indiscretions. Rafe's cheeks ached from laughter as the mountainous cousins drank and regaled him with stories of Bren getting them into every manner of trouble. Rafe let the men talk and mostly listened. 'Twas most the prudent action to prevent accidentally revealing too much about himself.

"Every lash from my father was a direct result of Bren's antics!" Nevan, the talker of the three cousins, explained. Bren smacked the giant on his arm.

"Ooch, nay! Ye got yourself into enough trouble on your own, old man!"

Bren's voice was almost a squeak. *Young, he had to be,* Rafe surmised. And his voice hadn't become a man's yet? A late bloomer, perchance? The youth was a puzzle.

Just as soon as the thought entered his mind, it left. Another round of drinks crossed their table. Whatever it was with the lad, Rafe found himself enjoying his company, and that of his drunk friends. Mayhap his travels to meet the Bruce would not be the miserable journey he'd anticipated.

***

Though Rafe had held his own as he conversed with the Fraser lad, under the glowering personas of his bodyguards, each moment he feared he might reveal his secret, that he'd expose his true roots.

And here, in Chisholm, where Rafe was certain the MacKay reputation preceded him, what welcome would he receive?

None. That's what he would receive.

Nay, less than that. These fair patrons and the innkeeper himself would throw him into the rain, with nary a kipper or bannock to keep him on his way. And these fine Fraser men drinking with him would be the first in line to toss him out on his arse. If they didn't beat him into the ground beforehand.

Most difficult for Rafe was recalling the landscape of the lands of which he was lying. He remained vague when discussing people and locations, relying on the stories of the Highlands as reference.

And one of the worst lies involved hiding anything about his parents. His father had died two years past, after a stilted life of imbibing too much ale, but the loss of a drunk father affected Rafe just as much as the loss of any father affected any son.

Rafe's mother had died in child bed, so he was an only child. That made the childhood untruths somewhat easier to bear. Rafe did send up a silent apology to his mother's spirit, that she may forgive him his lies. Still, he directed the conversation away from himself as often as possible.

The laddie, Bren, however, had no compunctions about sharing every detail of his life. The son of a local chieftain, he had a father, though his older brother and mother had died several years ago. Rafe racked his brain as the lad spoke, trying to recall any interactions he may have had with the Fraser clan — had he participated in a raid? In reiving cattle from them? But nothing in particular stood out, and Bren hadn't provided any specific details. If the MacKays did somehow contribute to those deaths, then Rafe had not been a part of those actions.

Still, he'd be guilty by association. So, he kept his mouth shut and his identity hidden. And while Rafe hated to admit it, reinventing himself on his way to the Bruce was both easy and pleasing. 'Twas nice not having dark looks or hard faces passing in his direction.

Any low notes in the conversation were skimmed over as the giants began to open up, with the help of tankards of mead, and by the evening, the men had shared rousing tales of the poor laddie. While some stories were strange, clipped, that overprotective nature

16

was a thread sewing all the tales together, and any story with any manner of hilarious ending were fair game, with or without the lad. Rafe's chest ached from laughing. The relaxing camaraderie among men after so long a time was welcome.

Something he'd not had, even from his own clan.

This 'twas what it was to be with those not bent on destruction.

Most strange was the way Rafe responded to the laddie. He had a sense of solidarity with the lad, and perchance something more. Almost like kin. But Rafe couldn't put his finger on it.

The lad's man thankfully paid for the evening meal, and after they ate, Rafe excused himself. 'Twas well into nightfall, and he did not relish setting out on the long journey toward Dumfries in the steady rain. He already had to spend precious coin on a room for one more night, then leave in the morn — storm or no. 'Twas all he could afford.

He bid Bren and his compatriots good eve and stumbled to his chambers. Falling into the bedding, he settled, sleep claiming him swiftly, knowing even as his mind drifted to the nether that he would regret his mead consumption come morning. Unlike his late father, Rafe was not one for nights of heavy drink.

He didn't give the peculiar laddie or his guards another thought.

***

The pounding at the door matched the pounding in his head.

Rafe pried one eye open, noting the dappled light in the room and the knocking at the door, both of which made his head throb.

The knocker didn't wait but entered Rafe's room. 'Twas the doe-eyed lass, looking much more the proper inn servant than she had in his bed two nights before.

She ported a tray with a large pitcher and a worn cloth. A fat cup sat on the tray next to the cloth.

"Ye drank yourself to oblivion yesterday," she tsk-tsked at Rafe, who was in no position to disagree. "I brought ye water to drink and a cloth to wash your face. I figured ye might need it this morn."

Placing her tray on the narrow table by the window, she faced Rafe, her enticing mouth pursed with disappointment at his drunkard state.

"Ye may want to avail yourself of the water quickly. Your friends from yesterday await ye downstairs."

At this, Rafe's head popped up from the coverlet. The movement was too much, and he waggled his hand under the bed, looking for the chamber pot. The woman kicked it to his hand, and Rafe emptied his stomach into the pot. She grimaced.

"My friends?" Rafe croaked, wiping at his chin. "What do ye mean?"

"The short laddie and his giant guards? They await ye at a table in the main room. Drink some water, wipe your face. Make yourself presentable. The young laddie seemed anxious to speak wi' ye."

Rafe nodded in understanding, and the lass departed, closing the door lightly behind her.

Why were they awaiting him? Had he revealed too much the night before? Truthfully, Rafe recalled little from their drunken conversation as the evening had worn on.

Swabbing away the remnants of vomit and sleep from his face, Rafe tried to wake up Then he filled the cup with water, drank in sloppy gulps, refilled it and drank again. Sated as best he could manage, he headed with trepidation toward the Frasers.

Chapter Two: The Frasers

THE LAD WAVED Rafe to the table where the giants gobbled a breakfast of rough bread, boiled eggs, and parritch. Watching the men tear through the food made Rafe's stomach roil, and he swallowed hard to settle his wame.

Bren held up an egg in offering, but Rafe declined it with a flap of his hand, instead opting for plain bread to calm his belly. He was certain his skin was green.

"'Twas a change in the weather last night," Bren told him. "We head out today, back home at Broch Invershin. Are ye heading south to join the Bruce?"

"Aye." Rafe's voice was rough, not quite recovered.

"Do ye ken where ye are going. Exactly? Where the Bruce is?"

Chewing carefully, Rafe shook his head. "Nay. I assume he's still at Dumfries, and once I make it close to Glasgow, I hope someone might be able to direct me."

"I have an offer for ye. We have some men returning from the Bruce's campaigns shortly. Ye can wait until they return in a fortnight's time, and then they can give you the Bruce's exact location." Bren took a large bite of his egg. "That way, ye are no' rambling about Scotland. Or if ye like, when more Fraser men depart for the Bruce, ye can accompany them. Whatever your preference."

Surprised at the offer, Rafe was silent and weighed his options. Heading to the Bruce's cause had only been a vague notion, an end point that encouraged him to leave the MacKays. He had no real plan of how to find the Bruce or what he might do once he got there. The pull to reach the Bruce's army had waned with each passing storm.

Taking time to collect himself, to learn where the Bruce was and figure out how long 'twould take to reach him? That prospect appealed to Rafe.

"Are ye asking me to go back with ye to your clan? Is there a place in your village I can stay? I dinna have much coin left."

An urge to be honest with the lad welled up within Rafe. As honest as he possibly could, that was.

Bren waved him off. "We shall find ye a croft, or ye might reside in the keep with the soldiers if my uncle and his advisers are open to it. Ye can bed down in the hall with the lugs here." Bren slapped the arm of the irritated-looking giant to his left, who didn't flinch.

Rafe found himself in a conundrum. Joining the laddie and his men was probably a foolish idea. Nay, not probably, it *was* a foolish idea. He didn't know these men, and they certainly did not know him. If his secret came out, he risked violence or worse.

Yet, he had no solid plan, only a general idea of finding the Bruce. He had few prospects and less coin as he made his way south. And Bren and his men might see it as an insult if he didn't accept the invitation. Then he'd have to come up with a believable lie for why he couldn't accept their offer. And he had already lied so much.

What finally convinced Rafe was wee Bren. Rafe missed the camaraderie of his clan, even as contrary as his clan may have been. Something of Bren and his clan spoke to Rafe's need to belong. In the end, foolish or not, that was what made up his mind.

"If it's nay a bother . . ." Rafe began, and Bren flapped his hand.

"Scots hospitality, my good man. Finish your meal and gather your belongings. Have ye a horse? If no, ye can ride with Kellan. The Frasers of Broch Invershin's stronghold is no' far to the southeast."

Bren clapped Rafe on his back, this time a powerful whack for such a slender hand. The young man's face lighted with bright eyes and a wide, excited smile, and Rafe surmised that another reason for the invitation existed under the surface. To Rafe, it appeared that the lad was trying too hard.

A frail lad under the sharp eyes of three giants? Most likely, the lad needed a friend as well. Rafe sighed wearily as he mounted the steps to his room to retrieve his sporran and *breacan*.

Friendship had quite a different meaning with the MacKays. The men of his clan fought and stole from one another rather than share a friendly meal. Lies and insults and backstabbing were the norm.

He didn't have a better plan, and Scots hospitality presented as a desirable option after days in the rain. Add to that the idea of forging a friendship . . .

Rafe wasn't sure he knew how to be a friend. Lying wasn't the strongest foundation for it, either. He could only hope his false pretense also made him a more affable man.

***

"What possessed ye to do such a thing?" Duncan roared at Bren in the privacy of their shared rooms.

The men packed up their few belongings, readying themselves for the ride to Broch Invershin of Loch Laro, when Duncan confronted Bren with the thought that burned in their minds. 'Twas their job to keep the Laird's child safe, and here Bren was, inviting danger home.

"What has ye so distraught?" Bren didn't look at Duncan as he tucked his dirk into his sporran. "He's just a lone man trying to make his way to the Bruce. I think ye'd appreciate the man for that."

"'Tis no' like bringing home a puppy," Nevan commented.

Bren didn't see the inherent dangers of bringing strangers to the keep, though Duncan and his men were more than aware. Ignoring the concern that the MacLeod man might be an English sympathizer, Laird Fraser's health had deteriorated over the last several years, a fretful situation that had every Fraser on edge. The Laird's brother and closest adviser presently led the clan.

Bren's father was Laird in name only, and while a few rumors circulated locally, the state of the Laird's health was not something the clan wanted to become widespread. Who knew what risks that could invite? Welcoming strangers into their lands when the Laird's health was already so precarious was a lousy idea indeed.

"I ken 'tis no' a puppy," Bren answered. He didn't hide the aggravation in his voice. "But we have a duty. I ken we've been at the receiving end of the MacKays for so long ye dinna trust anyone, but ye are big, strong men. If he's no' trustworthy, ye can deal with him."

His tone was nonchalant, and the giants' frustration showed on their faces. They weren't worried about *their* well-being.

"'Tis all well and good until the man is next to ye and pulls a knife afore we can reach ye. Or worse. We dinna have a care for ourselves, ye see. For ye, on the other hand . . ." Kellan didn't finish the sentence, but he didn't have to. Bren glared at his guard.

"Ye are implying I canna care for myself? That I am so weak and frail that I canna protect myself against one man with a knife and ye standing right behind me? Do ye think so little of me?"

Bren's words struck a chord in the men's chests, and they softened. 'Twasn't Bren's fault he was frail. That frailty, however, was their more immediate concern.

"First, 'tis your father to think of. Second, ye are weak and frail. Especially when compared to a man of that size. And what if the man learns —?" Nevan began, but Bren made a slicing movement with his hand, silencing the man.

"Naught. The man will learn naught. I have ye, our clan has ye, and we canna shut ourselves off from the rest of Scotland because one clan has wronged us so, or because my father is ill. We are no' moles, hiding in the ground. The Frasers are as hardy as my father's deer hounds. I will no' permit our losses to define us. We must always rise above such adversities. 'All my trust is in God' ye ken."

Duncan rolled his eyes to the sky at Bren's impassioned speech. Yet, hearing their clan motto come from so small a man chastised the giants, all of whom shrugged away, humbled. Their caution still lingered.

Nevan wasn't done speaking. "Ye need to take your own advice to heart," he mumbled under his breath. Bren heard but did not respond.

The Laird's son had the right of it, they knew. And Bren was more entitled than any of them to reject strangers, and he had done so in the past. To see him now try to welcome a stranger made them all question their scruples. Though the invitation to the MacLeod man didn't sit well with any of them, Clan Fraser rose above, doing whatever it took in the face of the worst atrocities.

Against their better judgment, the giants of Clan Fraser let the offer stand.

***

The rain had abated, but mucky roadways remained, and the horses picked their way over the rocky trail eastward. The journey was straightforward enough, yet the large men kept their attention on the trees and shrubbery surrounding them — wary and watchful. Rafe flicked his eyes over the landscape, trying to see what had the men so apprehensive. He saw nothing.

"Are ye always on edge when ye ride?" Rafe asked the Fraser man he rode with.

Kellan nodded.

"We've had a bit of a feud with another clan. Any time we are outside the walls of our keep, we are overly cautious."

Rafe went silent, and a sinking sensation overwhelmed him in a cold wave. He knew what clan feuded with the Frasers. His own. What exactly had happened between this clan and his own? The blood feud was years ago. He'd heard nothing that might lead to this sort of heightened caution.

After riding for some time, Duncan halted the horses, and they stopped.

"Let us give the horses a short break. This mud is difficult for them. And we can relieve ourselves. We should be at the keep by midday."

The Fraser men dismounted obediently, stretching their legs and backs after hours of rough traveling in the mud. Bren left Duncan's side, making his way toward a thick copse of trees. Rafe made to follow to relieve himself, only to be caught at his tunic collar by Duncan.

"Nay, laddie. Ye can relieve yourself over there, with Kellan and Nevan."

Rafe followed the direction Duncan indicated, and saw the Fraser men standing by the edge of the road, their kilts hiked up to their hips. Rafe shrugged and joined the other men, but his mind wandered.

If they were so protective of the slight lad, why did they let him ramble off by himself? Why take the laddie to an inn full of drunks? Why did the lad no' relieve himself on the side of the road with the rest of the men?

He'd just finished and was readjusting his plaid when a heavy hand landed on his shoulder. Duncan stood right behind him.

"MacLeod, I've been calling to ye. Why did ye no' answer?"

MacLeod. They were calling me by that name. And he had failed to respond. Not the best way to follow through on his subterfuge.

"Woolgathering," Rafe answered quickly, trying to cover himself.

Of course, the Frasers addressed him by his family name, not just his given name. 'Twas the way of men. He'd have to do better to pay attention to the MacLeod name and answer to it.

"Weel, quit your lolly-gagging and get ye done. Time to leave. We are but a few hours ride from Broch Invershin. Mount up."

Rafe waited by Kellan's horse, ready to mount after Kellan, when Bren stepped from the trees, patting down his plaid as he walked. He watched as Bren strode to his own horse under Duncan's stern, watchful gaze.

Rafe considered the behavior of the Frasers with the laddie as they rode on.

He must be sickly, Rafe concluded of Bren. For his small stature and the fierce protectiveness of the Fraser men, there could be no other reason. Even a youth, a Laird's bairn, should be treated as a man, expected to ride and hunt and work alongside the men — to behave as a man with a man's responsibilities.

If they lived in England, Rafe might think the laddie the foppish heir of a milquetoast nobleman, one who'd never done a real day's work in his life. Yet here, in the rough landscape of the Highlands, such character flaws were never tolerated. Not by any clan, not by any father, not by any kin. Illness, or something of that ilk, was the only plausible reason for the weak lad and his Highland guard.

Chapter Three: Broch Invershin

Invershin, West of Loch Laro, Northern Highlands

AGAINST THE CLOUDY skies, a stout brown-stone tower with an attached manse appeared on the horizon. A morning of riding had done its work on Rafe. Between the night of drinking and early rousing, several hours on the back end of a steed were enough for Rafe. Feeling the firm earth beneath his feet couldn't happen soon enough.

They passed through the postern gate into a small bailey surrounded by animal barns, a lean-to, women working on washing and collecting vegetables, and children gathering eggs and feeding chickens and goats. 'Twas a scene of unfamiliar tranquility.

A well-constructed stable sat off to the side, where the sturdy stable lads sat until Bren and Duncan rode into the yard.

Waves and "well-come" greeted them, and a tall man in a clean plaid approached with open arms. He bore a faint resemblance to Bren with the same bronzed hair, and from the warm embrace he gave the lad, Rafe easily made the connection that this man was close kin.

"Come, Bren. Your father awaits ye in the hall."

A happy glow settled into Bren's clear amber eyes at the mention of his father. Before departing, the laddie waved a hand at Rafe.

"Uncle, we picked up a stray. He is called Rafe MacLeod. He's on his way to join the Bruce. I offered him a bit of hospitality until our men return and can direct him where to meet up with the king's army."

The uncle nodded sagely and turned his attention to Rafe. Gone was the soft affection the man's face held for the lad.

"MacLeod, eh? And how are your kin to the far west? Did ye no' go with your kinsmen when they joined the Bruce?"

The man's stare held a hard edge. Bren may have extended Highland hospitality to Rafe, but his uncle's expression darkened to convey a measure of doubt as to that offer. Evidently, he didn't trust strange Highlanders who accompanied the slight laddie home any more than the giant guards had. Given Bren's position as the laird's son, the uncle's reluctance was, perchance, well-deserved.

"I had taken ill when my kinsmen rode for the Bruce," Rafe lied, hating how such mis-truths fell from his lips with ease. He'd left his clan to avoid the very behavior he was presently participating in himself, and he loathed it. He loathed himself.

"Ye look hale now." The uncle's eyes shifted from Rafe to Duncan. "Why did ye permit this?"

Duncan glanced over his broad shoulder, his expression hidden by his scraggly ginger-blond beard. His eyes did a quick assessment of Rafe — suffering from a night of excessive drink, a lack of sleep, and a morning of riding — and shrugged one shoulder.

"He's harmless. For some reason, Bren got on with him well enough. He drank with us and didn't seem improper." Duncan set a tempered gaze at the uncle, giving him a sign of who needed to be held accountable for the stranger.

The uncle's suspicious regard moved back to Rafe, and like Duncan, searched him up and down.

"Ooch, ye dinna look like ye could harm anyone. Duncan has a way of reading people. I'll take him on his word." He said the words without conviction, yet extended an arm. "I am Robert MacKinnon Fraser. Welcome to Broch Invershin of the Invershin Frasers."

Rafe, exhaling a relieved sigh, grabbed Robert's arm. His body shuddered with release, like he'd survived a gauntlet.

"Rafe MacLeod."

"I am the Laird's brother and adviser, and whilst the Laird is ill, chieftain in standing. Do ye have a place to stay, or did Bren offer ye shelter in the *broch*?"

He didn't sound pleased with the arrangement, and Rafe could hardly blame him. Fortunately, before he could answer, Nevan spoke up.

"He can bed down with us."

Robert settled his somber gaze on Nevan, then looked back at Rafe. That offer made the most sense — the guards could keep an eye on him if they kept him close. Nodding once to dismiss them all, Robert turned and left in the same direction as Bren.

"Will I meet Laird Fraser?" Rafe asked to no one in particular.

Kellan grunted. Duncan gave another of his one-armed shrugs. "If he decides 'tis a need."

Once they had dismounted, the stable hands scrambled to work, and Rafe was left behind in the yard, a throng of people circling his lonely presence. He watched as Robert and Duncan had words before going their separate ways. Rafe wasn't certain what he was supposed to do next. How might he bide his time until the Fraser men returned and could direct him to the Scottish army?

"Ye appear lost, man. Mayhap I can help ye?"

The soft voice came from behind, and he whirled around to find the epitome of Highland beauty. The buxom lass had fine, dark blonde hair and eyes as green as the glen on a summer morn.

Rafe raised an eyebrow at the woman. He knew he possessed roguish traits, and the appearance of this petite woman

32

coursed a shaft of desire through him. Bedding a kitchen maid on his first night as a guest at the keep, however, was not the most sensible decision. Rafe inhaled deeply, trying to cool his more base desires.

"Are ye daft? Do ye no' have a voice?"

Rafe clamped his mouth shut.

"Nay. Aye. I have a voice."

The fair lassie smiled in a wide grin. "Weel, then. I was watching as ye arrived. Ye must be famished. Do ye want some parritch?"

To emphasize, she held up a bowl near his nose. His aftereffects of a night of drinking had worn off. The scent made his mouth water and his stomach grumble. The fair lassie giggled.

"Weel, if ye dinna want to talk, your stomach does. Come with me to the kitchens, and I'll get ye a bowl."

With no other options present, and the sashaying backside of the comely lassie just as inviting as the parritch she carried, Rafe scrambled after her toward the kitchens.

She chatted away as they walked, introducing herself as Dawn, a kitchen maid, with a number of siblings whose names Rafe wouldn't be able to recall if asked later. He introduced himself under his alias, and Dawn gushed over his travels.

"I've no' left the Fraser lands," she told him as they entered the rear of the tower.

She gestured to a stool at the work-worn oaken table, and he sat. She continued to chatter as he ate, but he heard not a word. His mind kept flitting back to the wee Fraser lad, his intimidating guards, and the vexed-looking Robert Fraser.

Barring the attractive Dawn, Rafe again had the impression that accompanying the Frasers to their stronghold was yet another poor decision he'd made in a long line of poor choices.

***

"Why can I nay send ye on one task? All ye needed to do was deliver a message for me. Ye have asked and asked for something to do, not wanting to do the work ye should be assigned, and what do ye do?"

Fury burned off Robert as he paced around his study, glaring at the wee laddie who shrank in the cushioned chair. As of late, everything Bren did enraged or irritated his uncle. And Duncan. And Nevan and Kellan. And . . .

The only person he seemed to please was his father, and that was only because of the vile lie Bren was living and his father's crumbling faculties. Bren only pleased his father when Laird Fraser managed to remember who he was.

And Bren understood Robert's ire. Since his father's illness began to worsen, changing who the fine Laird was as a person, the less he recognized Bren. The surgeon and midwife had no name for it, no cure. The midwife, Riah, had told Robert and Bren that she'd seen it once in another man, a much more elderly man and not a Laird. The man never recovered and had died walking naked in the moorlands one winter night.

That prediction didn't bode well for Laird Kevin Fraser. And the more the illness ravaged his father, the more comfort Bren found in his lie. Until recently, when he wished his father might recall his own child.

"I've already reprimanded Duncan for his taking ye to the Inn. Such a foolish gesture. As 'tis, your father may have indulged this, this, whatever ye want to call it Bre—"

"Wheest!" Bren jumped from his chair at his uncle to silence him. Then he fell back on the chair, contrite. "My apologies, Uncle. I ken your concerns. Duncan only did what he thought best, given the inclement weather. And I will abandon the lie one day, soon. Ye've told me I must for more than a year. But right now, the lie suits my father, and it suits me. I've lived like this for so long, 'tis a warm cape that hides me from the world. Thank ye for indulging me."

As always, Bren's words touched Robert's heart. His close kin had suffered so great a loss over the past few years, with the horrendous murder of Bren's beloved older brother, the death of his mother, the deterioration of the Laird's health. If anyone were to understand and humor Bren's whims, 'twas Robert.

Having no wife or bairns of his own, he'd all but adopted his brother's children. The loss of Braden wracked him to his core. Then Maud's death had hurt Robert in a deep and unabiding manner — a pain he hadn't known possible. If his brother hadn't wed the lass years ago, Robert was more than ready to do so. Since she chose the older brother and position of Laird's wife, Robert was forced to pine for the lady from afar. Her death struck a black scar into Robert's heart that never fully healed.

Robert's gaze fell on Maud's youngest child, the one who resembled her so well 'twas uncanny. And his heart went out to the lonely bairn.

As much as he hated the weakness he had for his family, he forgave them and indulged them in any foibles. And this one, Bren, was a big one. For all Robert dressed in the role of a mighty warrior in his outer shell, his insides were soft as swan's down when it came to Bren.

"Aye, Bren. I ken that feeling. Right now, 'tis only ye and me to care for your father and keep everything on task. I just ask that ye have more of a care. There is a danger now that ye are older. Ye canna spend the night at an inn full of drunkards, even with your guards. Ye canna bring strange Highlanders from distant clans to the keep as ye would a lost puppy."

"I ken that, Uncle."

Frustrated, Robert rubbed a rough hand across his forehead.

"Ye are of an age. Six years of mourning, of hiding, have passed, of wearing your brother's clothes. Unless ye truly feel like —?" Robert struggled to put the idea into words.

Fortunately, he didn't have to. Bren flipped a hand at him.

"Nay, naught like that, Uncle." Bren picked at the ragged clothes, leftover from his brother Braden's belongings. "I feel safe. I feel nothing can harm me when I wear them. And it pleases Father."

Relief flashed over Robert's face. His voice calmed.

"As I said, ye are of an age. Perchance 'tis time to put your mourning and these childish fancies to rest and wear the clothing more appropriate for ye? Mayhap change your behaviors? The clan has been accepting, indulgent even, but now that ye're grown . . ."

Robert trailed off again. Bren understood what the man was trying to say. And his uncle wasn't wrong. He'd been saying it for nigh on a year. Bren was no longer a child. And Robert hadn't been the only one spending the last year or so hinting at dressing and behaving more appropriately. Perchance there was something to Robert's words. With how on edge Duncan had been on this last trip . . . Perchance 'twas time.

"But I don't know who I'm supposed to be," Bren admitted with a heavy tone.

Robert's face softened at the admission. "You can be anything ye want to be."

Yet Bren wasn't quite ready and told Robert that. "Can ye be patient? A bit longer?"

"Then why did ye bring the man home? To what purpose? Highland hospitality, my arse. Do ye ken how complicating that might be? Answer me that. Perchance there is another reason ye collected him like a lost pet?"

Bren bit at his lip. Robert's cautionary words were sound. Having an outsider too close, to learn about Bren, 'twas foolish.

"I'm intrigued by the man. We had strong conversation. He got on with Duncan and the men. Truly, I thought nothing more of it."

Robert raised one eyebrow, not fully believing. Bren may try to hide under oversized tunics and braies, but the coarse clothing only did so much. 'Twas obvious to the clan that Bren was scared and lonely.

"This was the last straw. I think 'tis time," Robert stated with finality. "Ye can do it one step at a time, but six years. My God, Bren. Our mourning must come to an end. And that means for ye as well. Ye canna grow and have the future ye should unless ye do. Figure out how ye want to start. Ye have the full support of the clan."

His uncle was correct, of course. But the comfort of Bren's position, could that be shed as readily as a tunic? Was he ready?

He stared into his dear uncle's face — the man who'd suffered gossip and ridicule, who cared for his invalid brother, who took on the weight of clan leadership, and did it all with good grace.

Bren didn't know how to start, but he silently vowed that he would.

He needed to emerge from his strange manner of mourning.

For his uncle.

For himself.

***

After the visit with Robert, which left him feeling rather like he'd been doused with a bucket of icy water, Bren was compelled to see his father. Dawn had entered the hall as Bren left Robert's study, and she waved Bren toward her.

"I am to visit your father. Do ye care to join me?" Dawn asked as she balanced a trencher of bread and parritch in one hand. Bren scooped it from her grasp.

"Aye. Is he awake, do ye think?"

Dawn lifted her slender shoulders.

"I have his midday meal and thought to relieve Anne for a bit. But your da does no' always ken the time of day, so he may not be ready to eat. He could well be napping."

Dawn knocked at the door before opening it. Anne's soft, caring face lifted at their entrance, a gentle smile crossing her lips.

"Dawn. Bren. How good to see ye both. I would say enjoy your visit, but alas, milord Kevin is asleep."

Anne flicked her head at the bed where Bren's father slept fitfully. His plaid blanket bunched up near his thighs, exposing a pair of pale, weak legs. Bren moved to the bed, covering his father's feet. 'Twas so different from the strong legs he recalled his father having only a few years ago. Such a great man, a powerful laird, withering away to nothing. Bren's chest lurched and bile rose in his throat.

Dawn spoke to Anne. "We will stay with him, feed him his meal when he wakes. Ye need fresh air. Take your time."

Anne nodded, set her sewing aside, and departed the room, her hair and skirts swishing as she exited.

Dawn placed the platter on the bedside table, then sat in the chair Anne had vacated. Bren sat on the edge of Kevin's bed, holding his frail hand and speaking in a low voice. A private conference with an ill father often meant talking while the older man slept.

"Uncle Robert and I spoke today, Father," Bren told his sleeping face. "We spoke of ye, of mother and Braden. He pointed out 'tis been nigh on six years. Six! Six years where I have lived like this. Hidden myself away. He said 'tis time to finish my mourning. But how can I finish when I see ye like this every day?"

A ragged sob caught in Bren's throat. He glanced over his shoulder at Dawn, but that good woman kept her own gaze lowered, focused on a piece of stitching. Bren was grateful for the pretense of privacy.

"I dinna ken what to do. But I fear Uncle is right. I dinna want to tarnish their memory, or the memory of ye. If I move on, accept who I'm supposed to be, is that an insult to ye?"

Kevin's only answer was a light snore. He slept the sleep of the innocent, and Bren had a flash of jealousy for it.

Sometimes, life was far too complicated.

Bren patted his father's hand before tucking it under his tartan. After a slight nod goodbye to Dawn, Bren stepped into the hallway and leaned against the cool stone. He pressed his palms against his eyes, forcing back the tears that threatened to fall.

Too many tears had been shed for the Fraser Laird and his broken family over the last several years. Robert's words echoed in his mind. Everyone was right.

'Twas time to take the advice of his betters and at least try to shake off the dismal mantle of his family's past.

***

Robert stripped to the waist, letting his plaid hang in loose flaps from his hips. The hearth was cold and dry, the air too warm for him to want a fire. A fat tallow candle on his table burned low. He dipped a swath of flaxen cloth into the water bowl and swabbed his lightly-furred chest and neck, relishing the cooling sensation as he wiped away the day's grime.

His thoughts danced around the ordeals of the past several hours, his concerns regarding Bren, his new MacLeod friend, and his brother's health consuming most of his contemplations. Some days his worries overwhelmed him, and he wondered at his ability to remain unwavering under the weight of these pensive matters.

Mostly he worried about Bren, who was of age and needed to assume responsibilities befitting the clan as the Laird's only child. How could Robert continue the conversation with Bren? Even today, Bren had provided halting responses at best. Might more demands from Robert convince Bren of what needed to be done, or push the bairn over the edge? How ready was Bren, how ready were they all, to put their mourning to rest?

A light knock at the door drew him from his reflections.

"Enter."

A mature, ethereal beauty slipped through the crack in the door, closing it behind her.

"Anne." Robert breathed her name.

A woman of good height, Anne was slender to the point of lanky, yet moved with an elegance that commanded a man's attention. Her rich, walnut-bark hair hung in long locks down her back, forming a cape around her shoulders. Her eyes were a scarce shade lighter than her hair and shimmered in the incandescence. Those eyes — not since Maud had a woman's gaze captured Robert's interest. Anne had become his saving grace as of late. His loins throbbed at the mere vision of her presence in his chambers.

"Robert," she answered and moved to him without hesitation.

He dropped his rag and opened his arms to embrace her. Her body and limbs were bony, fragile and breakable against his expanse of rippling chest and muscled arms. Anne's appearance, however, belied a strength he'd not known possible. Her patient dedication to Kevin, her skill in keeping him calm and contented amid the turmoil in his mind, spoke of a resilience most men didn't have.

And when she was with him in his chambers, in his bed, her strength became a softness, an enticing, inviting woman in whom Robert could lose himself over and over. She was a generous lover.

Wordlessly, Anne's mouth found Robert's, and he walked her backward to the bed. He gripped the neckline of her kirtle and tugged it down, exposing a high, supple breast to his needy lips. She cupped his head as he suckled. Shifting her hips, she pressed against his manhood bulging under his plaid. An animalistic groan vibrated in his chest, and he could deny himself no longer.

He yanked the kirtle to her waist, then moved his legs to drop his plaid to the floor. Anne's hand found his eager manhood, and Robert pulled her kirtle over the rest of her svelte body as he pushed her back to the covers.

Anne's thighs spread with willing ease, knowing he needed to have her, find his release, and he didn't hesitate. He thrust home, both of them clenching and moaning. Anne's legs wrapped around Robert's waist as he pumped and groaned. He didn't ignore Anne's own pleasure, and shifted to place a finger between them, rubbing at her hidden pearl until she lunged to meet him.

Robert built too fast and quickly thickened, spilling his seed deep inside her. Anne let out a rush of breath against his face. He remained above her, kissing her lips, her jaw, her neck, a steady appreciation of her body that she gave up for him. He longed to spend the night adoring every inch of her skin with his lips and tongue, thankful for the succor she offered.

"I needed ye tonight, Anne. How do ye always seem to know when I need ye?" His mouth moved to the bone below her shoulder. She shuddered at his touch.

"Ye need me every night. 'Twasn't a hard guess. Today, milord, your face was tight. Something happened after Duncan returned? Something with Kevin's bairn?"

"The child will send me to my grave. They brought a stranger home, if ye can believe such foolishness. 'Twas Bren's idea, and Duncan, the lout, permitted it. Something more significant is going on — as to why he was invited here and the man himself. Why did a man who was supposed to be joining the Bruce come here?"

His lips continued their feather light movements as he spoke, which made cognizant thoughts for Anne quite difficult.

"Bren is grown," she breathed against him. "Getting older. Mayhap this means things are finally changing."

Robert's head lifted above hers, his face hopeful.

"Do ye think? I asked Bren, and there is still some resistance. After six years of hiding away, do ye think time has healed some of those wounds? I've been mentioning it since last autumn."

"As have we all. Time and circumstances have changed, my dear Rob. Mayhap Bren is realizing that."

"We've had too much sadness for too long. Bren's been the focus of that, a reminder. If things are changing, then I am wont to welcome it. Mysterious stranger be dammed."

Anne's lips twitched with a playful smile as she pulled Robert's face down to hers.

"Life is always in a state of change. Let us rest so we can keep up with that change in the morn."

Robert lifted her with one arm, flipping the tartan coverlet out from under them and covering their bodies with it. They adjusted themselves under the warm blanket, Anne's lean frame nestled into Robert's muscular one, their faces close enough to share breaths.

Cocooned together, they left the larger concerns of the world outside the chamber door as they fell asleep.

Chapter Four: Secrets

THE FEISTY BLONDE kitchen maid Dawn gave Rafe a wink and a smile as she directed Rafe to where he could find a small loch for bathing. It'd been a fortnight or more since Rafe had really scrubbed his skin clean, and with the layer of filth on his skin, he was sure he looked and smelled like he lived in a barn. Dawn, however, didn't seem to care.

"Do ye need any assistance with your bath?" she offered suggestively.

Rafe sighed. 'Twould be too easy to find release between the tender thighs of this comely woman, but he needed to keep his focus. Clan Fraser had been more than accommodating, and the last thing he needed was to be found overstepping his bounds by swiving the kitchen maids. Control had never been his strong suit.

"While I do appreciate the offer," he told her as he eyed her from head to toe, "I must keep to myself. I thank ye for the directions."

She shrugged, non-plussed. "Suit yourself," she said, winked again, and returned to her work at the table.

Of course, she wasn't bothered by his rejection. Such a lovely and wanton woman undoubtedly had men lined up around the keep.

Rafe stepped gingerly around rocks and brush, pushing past the tree line to where Dawn indicated the loch was. As he made his way, he turned Dawn's offer over in his mind.

Any other time, he would have been more than willing to accept what she offered. Yet, since he'd left the MacKays, he tried to hold himself to a higher standard. Lassies like Dawn, however, were difficult to deny.

The loch came up amid a smattering of trees and grasses. The gentle lapping of waves was a soothing sound to calm his inner conflict. He stripped off his plaid and looked for a dry rock or bush to lay his clothing, when he noticed a set of worn braies, a tunic, and a plaid were laid out, taking up the best spot.

What —? Rafe snapped his head up to catch a swimmer in the water. From this distance, the diminutive figure in the waves appeared to be Bren. Thinking to join him, Rafe grabbed the hem of his tunic to lift it over his head when his eyes caught the sight of something impossible as Bren swam in the loch. Rafe froze.

Breasts. Bren had breasts. And not the type that men had when they consumed too much mead and rich food. First, that happened to older men. Second, these were soft and full, like a woman's.

Acting quickly, Rafe ducked behind the bush, hiding from what he just saw. 'Twas preposterous. Surely, he was mistaken — a trick of the light. A reflection.

He pressed his fingers between the branches of the bush and pulled them apart for another peek. This time, Bren had turned around and started to rise from the water, and had Rafe not already been crouched on the ground, he would have fallen over completely.

No manhood on the lad. Nay, Bren instead had a woman's mound, covered in a tuft of brown hair, darker than the hair on his head.

Not his head, *her* head. The gentle swell of the hip, dusky nipples on those full breasts, those long, slender legs . . .

Bren, the son of Laird Fraser, was a woman.

***

He blinked, then blinked again.

No wonder the Fraser giants were so protective of the lad. They were helping to keep Bren's disguise a secret.

Bren. That wasn't even his, *her*, real name.

So busy trying to make sense of these thoughts, he hadn't noticed that Bren, or whatever her name was, left the loch, droplets glistening on her soft curves, and was approaching her clothing,

And Rafe.

Panic rose in his chest. Searching around for a new hiding place, Rafe groaned inwardly. No other bushes were close enough, and even if they were, she would see him if he moved.

Instead, he remained where he was and bowed his head, praying the ground might open up and swallow him whole.

Bren reached for the clothing draped on the bush, and when she did so, discovered Rafe hiding gape mouthed behind it. She screeched, clutching her plaid to her naked, wet form,

"Rafe!" she shrieked. "What are ye doing? Why did ye follow me?"

Rafe scrambled from behind the bush, his hands up, desperate and placating.

"Nay! 'Twas no' like that! I just asked Dawn where I could wash, and she directed me here!"

The excuse sounded pathetic, and he hoped Bren bought it.

The dark fury in her eyes lightened, as did the strain in her muscles.

"Turn around, please," she instructed.

"Wait, what?"

She flicked her eyes down at her scantily covered body.

"I'd like to dress, aye?"

"Ooch, aye." Rafe jumped and spun around, presenting his backside to her. He listened as the rustling of clothing filled the quiet of the loch.

"Ye can turn around now," she said in a tart voice.

Rafe dropped his head and turned around, unable to meet Bren's eyes. How did he look at someone who was keeping such a secret, one that was inappropriately uncovered?

"I'm so verra sorry," Rafe began, but Bren stopped him.

"Nay. I couldn't keep it a secret forever. No' from ye at least, living at the keep. Most of the clan ken my secret. And according to my uncle, I need to stop dressing in this, anyway."

Her voice drifted off, as though 'twas difficult to speak on it. Rafe's gaze flicked up to hers. Once she was dressed, his brain had a hard time putting the young woman he'd watched swim in the men's clothing she wore. Freshly washed, she had no dirt on her face to pass as a scruffy beard, and her delicate beauty was captivating.

"Can ye tell me why? 'Tis no' every day I meet a man who's actually a woman."

Bren bit at her lip, brooding over his question. 'Twas bold to ask. Rafe had only known her for less than a sennight. A few nights of drinking, what did that mean with regard to trust? And he was lying about his own name! There was an inherent value to secrets. Mayhap he shouldn't have asked. She couldn't trust him at all, and she didn't even know it.

"'Tis complicated. My father, the Laird, lost a son — my brother Braden — years ago. Then my mother died of a broken heart soon after. I adored Braden. Followed him everywhere. Och, I started dressing in his clothing, to be closer to him, aye?" Her eyes glistened as she spoke, earthy pools that matched the loch behind her. "And to hide. 'Twas a place where I could just go away. Then I was lonely and trailed my father everywhere, as my brother had. Again, probably trying to be close to them both, missing a mother to shadow. But more than that. My father, too, he was so sad, ye ken?"

Rafe nodded. He knew where this was going. "Ye wanted to fill that space. Perchance make him happy again?"

Bren's face brightened. "Aye! 'Tis exactly it. But as a daughter, I could no' do that. If I pretended to be a son, 'twas easier for everyone. And my father did seem to appreciate the effort. Since he didn't ask me to stop, I didn't."

"Surely, it's been years. And ye still dress —?" Rafe wore his confusion in his features. For a child to do so was endearing, but for a young woman, 'twas a bit strange.

"Familiarity. And freedom," she answered almost too quickly. "Do ye think I could enter an inn, drink mead with the men, and blend in if I donned a gown edged in gold? Wove flowers and ribbons in my hair? In this, I can ride a horse, even wield a sword, a wooden one, if badly. And I dinna have to fend off assertive suitors who quest for my hand for less than noble reasons."

Rafe burst out laughing, the image of a slight lad lifting a sword weighing half a stone. But why did she want to carouse with men? That question went unanswered.

"Ooch, a small sword. And a dirk," she added in a petulant tone, the lines of her chin jutting up to him.

Waving his hands in front of him, Rafe gained control of his laughter.

"My apologies. Ye are correct, a smaller sword ye could well wield, I concede. And a dirk for certain. And your father let ye continue?"

"Once I started, I guess we grew used to it. 'Twas . . . comfortable. For us, 'twasn't strange, aye?"

There most assuredly was more to this story, Rafe kenned that well enough. And though he thought it odd, Rafe was familiar with the way continued actions become acceptable habits, his own clan a pristine example of *that* philosophy. He also recognized the comfort of hiding one's true self.

"If ye are done bathing," Rafe decided 'twas safer to change the subject, "do ye mind if I have a swim?"

"Ooch! Nay, please do. The chill of the water is invigorating."

She stepped to the side, gesturing to the shimmering water with her arm. Rafe stepped past her, then paused.

"Can I ask ye one more thing?"

She shrugged. "Why no'? Ye ken my biggest secret now."

"What is your name? Your real name, I mean?"

She stared at him again, weighing the implications of her answer.

"Brenna. My name is Brenna Morgan MacKinnon Fraser."

Rafe bowed low, like a prince in a foreign court.

"Pleasure to meet you, Brenna," he told her before turning toward the loch and stripping off his tunic to swim.

***

Once the shock of discovery wore off, a measure of relief flooded Brenna. 'Twas a trial to keep up the appearances of being a man, the mannerisms — 'twas tiring, especially when around someone new. To be caught, able to reveal her true self, was freeing. Perchance more freeing than dressing in her brother's clothing, as she'd suggested to Rafe. And that was not a sensation she'd expected to feel.

At first, she feared Rafe had other, less-than-gentlemanly intentions at finding her disrobed. His dramatics in allowing her to dress with his back turned made her nearly laugh out loud. Such a proper young man. Surprising even, which lightened the mood at his discovery.

And he was so easy to talk to, just as he'd been at the inn. While she was initially taken aback at his inquiries of her disguise, the answers to his questions rolled off her tongue. Years had passed since simple conversation set her at ease.

The men of her clan held her at a distance, tolerating her but not accepting her, as she wasn't a man, and 'twas improper to get too close to the Laird's daughter.

The women of the clan didn't understand her, and rarely engaged her in any conversation, preferring to keep their distance. They saw her as soft in the head, like her father. Even the outlandish Dawn could be reticent when it came to Brenna.

It had been easier to pretend to be someone else than deal with the loss of her brother and her mother, in addition to the constant reminder that she was the daughter of the laird who lost his family. She could be anyone she wanted, not the woman who lost a dear mother and a brother she adored.

Rafe seemed interested, intrigued even, over her disguise, not horrified or angry at her deceptions. And his formal introduction, complete with a bow, brought a smile to her lips and a surge of joy in her chest — a feeling long gone.

When was the last time she experienced any sense of true joy? Not since before her brother or mother had died. Or since her father failed to recall his memories of her. Or forget who she was entirely.

To Brenna, Rafe saw her for who she really was, men's clothes or not.

'Twas a divine feeling, to be sure.

Brenna feigned as though she was returning to the keep. However, she decided that what was good for the goose was also good for the gander. Curiosity got the better of her. Why not watch Rafe as he washed? 'Twas only fair after all.

By the time she'd found a decent hiding spot behind a well-aged tree and a scrub of brush, Rafe had removed his tunic, dropping it on the grass near the loch's edge. The defined muscles on his back danced in the late afternoon sunlight. 'Twas a back that exuded power, muscles developed from years of use, hard work, and sword wielding.

She scolded herself for spying, but isn't this what her uncle and everyone else wanted? For her to behave like a woman rather than a lad? Did women spy on and appreciate the view of half-dressed men?

Then he dropped his braies onto the tunic, and she sucked in her breath. Inappropriate behavior be damned. The man resembled a god carved from granite — rigid and chiseled to perfection. Brenna's reaction to him was potent and immediate.

She'd seen naked men before, from a distance or in horseplay around the keep, but this — a well-muscled stranger who didn't know her? It was almost taboo.

Especially since his long legs and taut, curved buttocks were readily visible as he walked into the water. The muscles on his backside rippled as he waded into the low waves of the loch. He was in his full glory, a hardened Highlander with a warrior's body, and Brenna relished the view.

Rafe waded into the water up to his thighs when he suddenly turned, splashing at his chest as he walked in deeper.

The side view of his manhood was not what she'd expected. After taking in the sight of his manly shaft, which protruded from a thatch of hair the same midnight hue as the locks on his head, she slapped her hands over her mouth to cover the squeal she emitted and ducked behind the brush. What if he heard her?

Peeking over the top of the brush, Brenna saw Rafe was now waist deep in the loch, dunking his head back as he scrubbed at his chest.

Astounded at her scandalous conduct, she took advantage of his distracted attention and tip-toed away from the tree toward home, feeling lighter than she had in a long, long time.

***

The grass was refreshing under Brenna's bare feet, providing a cushion against any rogue, sharp stones that she might have stepped on. She carried her *breacan* as she walked, relishing the gentle breeze and the sense of freedom she experienced in loose clothes and bare legs.

Having worn braies so much over the past years, with only a kilt here or there, Brenna found she missed the liberating movements of skirts every so often.

Glancing over her shoulder to the last view of the loch, she wondered at what she'd missed. Six long years, but what else could she have done? When her brother had died (*was murdered,* she corrected herself), she'd thought the world was ending, and tried to hide in her parent's room. But then her mother took to bed and didn't rise again, and there was nowhere left to hide.

Braden had always told her to come to his room if she required anything, needed assistance, and his dancing eyes and easy smile had welcomed her every time. Braden's room was a place of sanctuary, and once her mother died, she ran to that sanctuary. His tunic was thrown over his trunk, left over from when he'd worn it last. It had smelled of her stinky brother when she slipped it over her torso. In her mind, 'twas still warm from his body. And she wanted that feeling of closeness never to leave.

She didn't realize that she'd live in that moment for years.

Then, in childlike willfulness, she wanted to shorten her name, make it more like her brother's, feel closer to him in his absence. Becoming Bren worked well. Until it didn't.

The minute she bumped into easy-going Rafe, the pretend life Bren had lived was no longer important. No longer *right* for her. In that minute, she regretted not wearing a fine kirtle or having her hair sweeping her back. A surging thrill deep inside her chest had made her swoon.

'Twas why she'd lost her balance when she "bumped into him" at the inn. Not that she'd share *that* secret with anyone.

And 'twas why she asked him to join them that night. 'Twas why she invited him home. The entire ride back to Broch Invershin, she'd wracked her brain, searching for a way to show or explain who she really was, while hiding her truth out of that eternal anxiety that oppressed her each day.

Her guards, however, made any manner of hinting at her true identity impossible. They took their vocation too seriously, especially when she dressed as a lad. And she understood their caution — far too much could go awry if she were discovered. The danger was too great. Women had been called witches for less. Her guards may have indulged her childish whims, but they didn't permit those whims to lead to destruction.

And she had used that to her advantage. Years of having them following her around led to complacency. Duncan was the most ardent, but it didn't take much time for Kellan and Nevan to grow trusting, lax in their guardianship. Their permissive behaviors allowed her much more freedom than her uncle, or Duncan, would have cared for.

If they found out.

A sly smile crossed her lips.

When she was younger, her unchaperoned adventures meant play sword fighting with the other youngsters of the village, sneaking off to pick flowers or chase butterflies, or to have private time by herself. Having a shadow all the time was trying. But since she'd stayed out of trouble, her guards had grown bored and a bit sloppy.

Lately, though, as she'd grown older, even while under the guise of dressing like a lad, Brenna had noticed young men in the clan not engaging with her the same way. She was not a child, and they were more stand-offish. Duncan and her guards began giving her more privacy, keeping their own distances.

She dropped her eyes to her chest. It didn't take a learned man to know why. Why her uncle had started encouraging her to come out of her hiding and dress in gowns and kirtles. Why Duncan and men from the clan didn't come too close. What had been an indulgence when she was a child was now wildly inappropriate.

And her clan would be forgiving of her false identity for only so much longer. It had worked to prevent rogue suitors from abusing her father's illness and Brenna's fragile state as a way to trap her into marriage. But her uncle now led the clan with a strong hand, and Brenna was sure she'd overstepped her clan's threshold of patience long ago.

As much as she'd fought against it, Brenna had blossomed into her full womanhood. She'd caught reflections of herself in the mirrored surface of the still, early morning loch and saw the delicate lines of her face, the thrust of her breasts against her shift, the curve of her hips that loose braies and flaps of plaid just couldn't hide.

Her insides told her she couldn't hide anymore. The handsome grin of the miller's son, the soft eyes under bushy blond eyebrows of the boy she saw in the village — Brenna started noticing them in a way she hadn't when she was a bairn. She'd even tried to hug the miller's son when he wasn't paying attention.

And she found she enjoyed it. She giggled to herself. She sounded like a young lass just discovering lads, instead of a full-grown woman.

She hadn't wanted to be a lad. Just dress as one — to feel closer to her brother, to pretend the past six years were something that happened to someone else. It was easier to endure dressed in her brother's clothes.

Six years. Six years of mourning her mother. Of missing her brother. Of sadness over her father's declining health.

Her uncle encouraged her to let the past sleep. To leave behind these childish whims of hiding in her brothers' clothes, his room, and resume her life. To step into the life she was meant to have.

When she was younger, Robert had asked if she wished to leave that person behind. Perchance he'd seen that she was struggling with the woman she'd become and the childish past that she was running from. And his kind voice told her he would honor the decision she'd made.

But now she was an adult. 'Twas time to come to terms with the past and accept her role in the clan. Those horrible events had happened to Brenna, to her, and she'd had ample time to put those gruesome memories to rest. The larger, looming question was, how to do that? After so long, she was Bren to most of her kin. How difficult would the transition back to Brenna be?

She flicked her gaze over her shoulder once more. Rafe and the loch were too far away for her to see, but in her mind's eye, the image of that hardened warrior appeared before her eyes just as if he were right there.

If she were to resume her life, shed her pretending to be Bren as she shed her brother's clothing, she might find a husband, become a wife, a mother, and continue the line that the MacKays tried so fervently to eliminate. She might find a man with raven hair, flashing eyes, and a broad chest.

A man like Rafe.

Chapter Five: Harsh Truths

WHEN RAFE RETURNED to the keep later in the day, his hair was still dripping wet, but the refreshing cleanliness was invigorating. He made the judicious decision not to seek out Brenna. They must continue the conversation, that he vowed to himself, but now was not the time. Too many people, too much activity, and too much drinking for any worthwhile discussion.

And he was too intrigued for anything less than a private conversation. Her desire to live in disguise fascinated him. Rafe hadn't been able to get the image of her in the loch, droplets coursing down her slick, fair skin, from his mind.

Thankfully, the loch had been rather frigid, and he was able to cool the fire that had ignited in his loins.

Why did she occupy his thoughts so? She'd been a conundrum since they first met. *It had to be her odd dress and manners.* At least, that was what Rafe told himself.

Another lie to add to the many he was presently collecting.

Rafe entered the main hall where tables were set for the evening meal. He found an empty seat at a bench at the rear of the room. Then he let his eyes pan the hall and take in his surroundings.

Brenna sat by her uncle at the head table near the hearth. She had resumed her mannish costume, her short hair slicked back in shining waves and her tunic loose and neat. No stained tunic for dining in the main hall.

Her father, Laird Fraser, was absent from the hall — or rather, Rafe didn't see anyone who could be her father sitting at the table. But Brenna's uncle drank with aplomb, keeping up with his men. The man was trying to drink his troubles away, which didn't quite match with the man he'd met when Rafe first arrived. With Robert's burdens of the clan, a niece who hid herself in a lad's clothing, and no male to carry on Laird Fraser's lineage, Rafe understood the man's need to drink away his pains.

His eyes flicked back to Brenna. Her family was so broken, even the only daughter abandoned her identity to pretend to be a son. It pained his heart in a deep and unabiding way, and Rafe wasn't sure why.

He had liked the young man, Bren, well enough — the lad had temporarily filled the role of the younger friend, or even a brother, to Rafe. Now knowing Bren's true identity, Rafe's emotions roiled in his head. Could he still be a friend to the young man who was really a woman? An attractive one at that? A friendship of that sort was surely inappropriate. Why did she remain hidden if most of her clan knew her secret? And what of Rafe's strange affections for Brenna the woman? Those could not be explained as readily.

As soon as he had that thought, another one made his brain ache all the more. Here he was, judging the young woman for her decision to hide her identity, and what was Rafe doing? The same thing. The MacKay name was detested in this clan for their vicious slights. Hiding his own true identity under the MacLeod clan made him no better than the dear lass who was trying to please her father and hide from her pain.

In fact, the more Rafe considered it, the more he realized his own deception was worse. He had no noble cause for disguising his identity. He was only trying to avoid retribution and lying more and more to do so. Brenna's reason was full of heartache and indulgence. Rafe's was self-serving.

These dark ruminations sent his mind to an even darker place, and he consumed one drink after another, starting with mead and progressing to the whiskey that flowed more freely than was prudent. No wonder his father had drank. It numbed pain and somber thoughts.

The other Fraser men ignored him, perchance sensing Rafe was not in a good place, or they were not comfortable with the stranger. They passed the cups his way without comment. Rafe took advantage of that flow. Soon his somber thoughts had fled and were replaced with appreciative glances at the nubile kitchen maids, the lovely Dawn in particular. Another way to escape pain.

He needed a distraction from Brenna and his own melancholy and wildly inappropriate notions, and this woman fit the role. How better to forget his conflicting emotions than with a willing lass?

Blonde tresses and light green eyes, and plying Rafe with pitcher after pitcher. Even in his drunken state, Rafe didn't miss the cloying looks or lingering touches when she brought him mead. A distraction indeed.

He'd not been with a woman since the kitchen maid at the inn. And his confounding thoughts about Brenna only stirred him more. He missed that connection, the meeting of skin and souls amid panting and pleasure. Dawn had made it clear she was more than willing.

When Dawn stepped into the dim hall near the kitchens, Rafe didn't hesitate. He rose from the bench on unsteady legs. Dawn was just inside the hall when he entered.

"I was hoping ye'd find me here," she murmured in a sultry tone, twining a blonde lock with one finger. She pressed her other hand under her ample breasts, offering them up just as she had offered him mead.

Only what she offered now was more tempting.

Rafe leaned into her, resting his arm on the cool stone wall above her head.

"Oh, did ye now?"

She didn't shy away from his drunken interest; in fact, she inhaled, pressing the generous swells of her breasts even closer to his appreciative eyes.

"Are ye only going to look?"

Her question was suggestive, and Rafe took her up on that suggestion. He lowered his face, closing the gap between them until his lips brushed hers. Dawn parted her lips in response, inviting his tongue to ravage her mouth. He cupped her head with his hand and accepted the invitation.

He moaned into her mouth, his cock rising under his plaid. But 'twasn't this kitchen maid who was on his mind as he kissed her — a bronze-haired lass danced in his thoughts. Dawn reached her hands around his back, clutching at the hard globes of his backside, encouraging him, urging him on. He lifted his lips from Dawn's, his head a mass of confusion. What was wrong with him?

The patter of footsteps and a soft "oh!" interrupted them. Rafe didn't pull away, only twisted his head to see who the voyeur was.

He shot straight up when he saw Brenna in her men's costume, staring at his and Dawn's enthusiastic embrace.

"Brenna!" he exclaimed, seeing the woman who hid under her manly clothes. When her eyes widened, he realized his mistake. Two mistakes.

He cut a slow look of shock to Dawn, who had slapped her hand over her mouth when he said Brenna's name. Did Dawn know Brenna's secret? Of course, she did. Was her surprise over the fact that Rafe knew?

Rafe took one slow step away from Dawn and returned his gaze to Brenna.

"I'm so sorry. I did no' realize . . ."

Not only did a flush in dismay at breaking Brenna's confidence heat his skin, he also had a sense of shame that she should have found him in a compromising position with a kitchen maid.

Brenna hugged her arms around her waist. Rafe extended a desperate hand to her.

"Brenna . . ."

She turned and ran back the way she'd come.

Rafe hung his head in defeat. She had entrusted him with such a considerable secret, and here he was, letting drink and his cock take control, and he exposed her. 'Twas not his place to out her, and here he was doing such a thing. She'd never trust him again.

What manner of man was he, denouncing the Fraser trust this way? Perchance he deserved the MacKay name.

"Rafe."

His name echoed in the darkened hallway. He swiveled his head around to Dawn, her pale face stark against the shadowy stone.

"How did ye ken? Bren keeps a tight knot on his, uh, pretense?"

"'Twas an accident." He brushed an agitated hand through his hair. "I saw her swimming in the loch, and she confided in me. Now here I have broken that confidence."

Dawn tipped her head up at Rafe and laid a light hand on his arm.

"Dinna fret over much about Brenna. *Bren*. Most of the clan kens why she dresses and behaves as she does. Many of us in the clan see the benefit — to protect her from falling into the wrong suitor's clutches, o'course. And for her father. He's gone sick in the head, and it helps him believe that his son is still alive in some way. He gets confused sometimes. The clan doesn't talk about it, but we all ken. His brother and advisers rule the clan behind Laird Kevin's back. Brenna doing what she does keeps the Laird calm and compliant. And eases his pain, and her own. She's well loved, so we go along. Is that so wrong?"

She was looking at him for validation. To many, it might seem strange. As an outsider, he had a different perspective. He could understand Dawn's concerns. From the outside, it seemed as though the clan was daft, even weak, to permit such an atrocity — a woman dressing as a man.

And add an ill father to boot. Dawn had said "soft in the head," which could be any manner of unfortunate illness. Rafe recalled his own father before he'd died. Even while the man was drunk, Rafe had adored his father. Would he had done any less? And to keep the lass safe from predatory suitors? 'Twas even sensible. Mayhap her disguise was not as curious as he first assumed.

"Eventually she will have to stop, aye? Does no' her father want to see her wed? Taken care of?"

Dawn cast her eyes down at her skirts.

"Mayhap. But we dinna ken what her father knows is real or no' and his health is worsening. We dinna ken how long the man may live. Ye are nay wrong. Soon she must shed her childish behavior and assume her responsibilities in the clan. We've been telling her that for a while. That time will come nigh soon. For now, we let Brenna do what she does."

'Twas a sad story, a tale that seemed pulled from ancient times. A frail father. A dead son and mother. A daughter willing to do anything to please her da. Brenna's actions, if sanctioned by her clan, were not so nonsensical after all.

Rafe and Dawn stared at each other from opposite sides of the hall. The moment between them had passed, his interest in her fading, her duties in the kitchens beckoning. He bowed cordially and bid her good eve, then left her to find his own bed for the night.

***

Brenna rushed through the hall, ignored by the drunken sots loitering among the benches and tables. She burst through the doors into the open air of the night and halted. She was upset, on the verge of tears, and she didn't fully understand why. As such, she wasn't sure where she even wanted to run away to.

The rustling of leaves in the wind answered her question, and she picked her way through thick grass and shadowy rocks to a low stone wall at the border of the kitchen gardens. A gentle mewling from the wall's edge attracted her attention. Bending toward the sound, Brenna discovered one of the Broch mousers, a kitten really, cowering in the gardens.

Making a low clicking sound with her tongue, Brenna managed to convince the kitten to come forth and sniff her fingertips, and Brenna scooped up the wee beastie. 'Twas no more than bones and orange and black fur. That and a fierce mewling as Brenna scratched at its neck.

'Twas something peaceful in cuddling a kitten, an action Brenna didn't get to indulge in often since the kittens scrambled about, hiding during the day and chasing mice and other vermin at night. Downy fur tickled Brenna's chin and irritated her nose.

Once the kitten settled, snuggled into Brenna's neck, its contented purring vibrated across Brenna's chest. Finding this kitten to cuddle when she was strangely despondent helped to calm her tumultuous emotions plaguing her chest and mind. How could one fret when holding pure contentment?

A crunching sound behind her made her turn and peer over her shoulder. Dorcas, another kitchen maid, stepped from the gardens.

"I do no' mean to frighten ye," she apologized to Brenna. "I heard someone out in the yard and thought to investigate. Are ye well?"

'Twas a common question. Few in the keep understood Brenna's shifting emotions, even as they were sympathetic to her pain. And since they didn't understand, one of the first questions anyone asked her was how she was feeling that day. And the question only added to her complicated frustrations.

"I've had so many feelings as of late. Ones I dinna understand."

Dorcas cleared her throat and settled onto the wall next to her. "Do ye mean the ones ye had for the miller's son? The lad I saw ye leaning against last spring behind the barn?"

"Dorcas!"

Brenna's hand flew to her mouth, and Dorcas laughed at her discomfiture.

"Ooch, no one else saw ye. Only me."

A deep sigh pulled from Brenna's chest. "Nay. No' the miller's son. 'Tis someone else. I dinna ken him well, and after the past six years . . ." She let her words trail off. She was truly wrestling with the emotions warring inside her. What was happening?

"What would ye say to him, this man ye dinna know well?" Dorcas asked, her interest in Brenna's mystery man piqued. 'Twas obvious Brenna was talking about the MacLeod man.

"Weel, I should like to get to know him, of course."

"And?"

"And what?"

"Surely a man who is worth knowing is deserving of some attention."

"Dorcas!"

"Is it any less than ye gave the miller's son? Or did ye no' care to wed —?" Dorcas paused, not wanting to overstep. Brenna was such an enigma. Who was to say what the lass wanted?

"Nay, I care. I just dinna know the man."

Dorcas shook her head as she patted Brenna's leg.

"That has no' stopped many a man. Or woman. Ye can know a man for years and he will be as large a deceiver as he was the day ye met him. Ye can know a person your whole life and they will still betray ye. But ye can know a man for hours, or days, and he can be your match. And here ye have a man ye seem to care for. Shouldn't ye at least try to do something to get to know him?"

Dorcas let the question hang in the air. Like the rest of the clan, she was unaware of Brenna's meeting Rafe at the loch and their light banter. If she did know, the Good Lord could only guess what words the woman might spew then.

"Are ye afraid because he met ye when ye were dressed as a lad? That he may think something, uh, untoward about your dress?"

"Nay," Brenna responded, shaking her head. Nay, Rafe did not seem to have an issue with her dress, or lack thereof. "I mean, I dinna think so. I dinna believe he cares over much. Won't it be curious if I suddenly change my clothes and stop pretending?"

"Mayhap, but a nice curiosity. I think ye are hesitant to trust anyone, unless 'tis your uncle. Ye've been closed away from the world for so long, perchance ye are afraid to open up? To come out from hiding? Afraid to trust in a world that has abused ye so harshly?"

Dorcas leaned across the length of the stone wall that separated them and embraced Brenna in an awkward hug. The kitten wiggled in Brenna's grasp. Freeing itself, it jumped to the ground and disappeared into the gardens.

"Mayhap ye need to give the world another chance. 'Tis obvious that the world is giving ye another chance."

Brenna rested against Dorcas, seeking comfort. "Why do things have to change?"

"'Tis the one constant in this world, dearie. How droll would it be otherwise?"

Dorcas disentangled herself from Brenna, kissed the top of Brenna's head, and strode off towards the kitchens. Brenna remained in the cool evening, trying to make sense of everything Dorcas had said. She picked at her worn braies.

At least Dorcas hadn't told her to put on a gown.

***

Rafe found his bed, a flat pallet amid several snoring Fraser men in a sleeping area off the main hall. After the shock of what he'd learned today and all the mead he had imbibed, he'd assumed that sleep would find him with ease.

He was wrong.

Instead, he stared into the darkness, as vague shadows and the guttural sounds of men sleeping attracted his senses, keeping him awake.

No, 'twasn't those senses that denied him sleep. 'Twas the vision of a fair, bronze-hair lass with fragile eyes.

Rafe hadn't even had the opportunity to think clearly regarding what had transpired. Between his work, his bath, his discovery, his drink, and his minor interlude with Dawn, he'd found it difficult to focus at all.

Any other time, he'd have had his way with the blonde Dawn lassie. While he may have not taken her right there in the hall, Rafe had no doubt that, under any other circumstance, she'd be in his bed right now.

That one distinction, however, plagued his thoughts.

Brenna. How long had she dressed in men's clothing? Long enough for the clan and her kin to call her by her nickname. Long enough for everyone to accept it as normal.

But was it normal to hide like that?

Rafe's chest burst with a sardonic laugh. Who was he to judge? Other than the fact he didn't change his mode of dress, wasn't he doing the exact same thing? The only true difference was Brenna had been doing it for much longer, apparently. And unlike Rafe, Brenna and her odd quirks were received by her clan.

If Rafe had tried to change who he was with the MacKays, he would have been shunned. Turned away, even. He envied Brenna and her clan that accepted her peculiarity so readily.

The reasoning, though, that Dawn provided was weak. The clan accepted it because they loved her? They acknowledged that she wanted to feel closer to her brother and please her father in some way? Those explanations didn't appear sound.

Well, feeling closer to the brother — that made sense to Rafe. His father kept one of his mother's kerchiefs tucked away in his trunk, and removed it, sniffing it lightly, when he was deep in his cups and missing Rafe's mam.

But the other excuses Dawn gave? Nay, Rafe told himself. There had to be something deeper going on. He knew the Laird was ill, the Uncle led the clan in his stead, the brother was dead, and Rafe had heard little of the lass's dead mother. The Frasers were a strange puzzle where Rafe was only permitted to see part of it at one time.

Secrets, Rafe well knew, didn't stay hidden. Look at how easily he learned Brenna was a woman. If there were any other family secrets, Rafe was sure to unearth them before he continued his journey to the Bruce's army, if he desired.

Having met Brenna, though, that prospect of leaving suddenly appeared less inviting.

Chapter Six: The Hunt

THE POUNDING IN HIS head the next morning was his punishment for drinking too much mead and a lack of sleep the night before. The last time he'd drunk thusly, he ended up with the Frasers. Mead was a devil for him, giving him pleasure and courage in the evening, then hammering his head and wame in the morn, coupled with a tinge of regret.

He'd have to quit the drink. Over-imbibing was not a positive trait, was strongly frowned upon by many, including the church, and it reminded Rafe far too much of his previous life with the MacKays. Of his father. If he detested it so much, why did he continue the practice?

Because he was broken. He hated to admit it to himself, but it was unmistakable. He lacked character in many ways, not only in his drinking. And here he was, living off the benevolent favor of a clan so caring of its people that they put up with a facade of the Laird's daughter. He was a stain on this clan. Though he had planned to stay until the Frasers returned with news of the Bruce, Rafe doubted that continued to be a sound choice. Perchance 'twas time to move on. He might make up a polite excuse for leaving early.

He rolled his sickly body off his pallet at the rear of the room, then rolled right back on with a groan.

But not today. He wasn't moving anywhere this day. Rafe closed his eyes against the pale light and hoped that, when he opened them again, his body wouldn't protest as much.

***

Another pounding, and Rafe pried one eye open. He feared 'twas his head again, but this time 'twas feet stamping on the rushes beside his head. He opened his other eye to find Brenna, dressed in her Bren disguise, trying to rouse him. Kellan stood next to her, a grin plastered on his wide face. He was enjoying Rafe's torture.

"Come, man," Brenna demanded. "We are going hunting. Antlered stags were sighted in the grove nearby, enough meat to feed a clan! Time to earn your keep."

That explained her brother's clothing. Not that she'd wear it anyway, but hunting in a woman's gown was not ideal. Running, riding, skinning, 'twere tasks predisposed to men's clothing. Rafe needed to practice not exposing her secret on this hunt he was being pressed into joining.

He of the mocking grins remained quiet. Kellan was Brenna's muscle, and Rafe had no option but to say aye. Kellan wouldn't accept any other answer. The mountain of man had scorned Rafe from their first meeting — Rafe wasn't going to grant the giant any reason to give him grief now.

A skin of water smacked him in the head, a gift from Kellan to help lessen his hangover and set Rafe straight for a day of hunting. Rafe nodded his thanks, drank deeply, and finally rose to his feet with a groan. 'Twould be a long day indeed.

The pale sunlight provided a perfect day to spend in the woods. The air was fresh, even heightened as the excitement of the hunt flowed like weak wine among the men. More than once, Rafe cut his eyes to the Laird's daughter who today called herself Bren. Seeing her in a circle of men, leading the hunt, including Duncan and Nevan who had joined them, shocked Rafe to his core. The scruffy appearance of a lad was so contrary to the vision of the water nymph he saw yesterday.

Aye, she had a contingent of Highland men who served as her personal guard, but knowing what danger existed on something like a hunt, how did her father, or better yet, her uncle who still had all his senses, permit such behavior?

Her circle of guards was steadfast in their duties most of the time Rafe saw her. Except for their time at the loch, Brenna was never more than an arm's length from any one of the ferocious-looking men. Which then begged the question to Rafe, how had she eluded them that day she went swimming? Even as they rode hard after their prey, the men managed to keep their horses abreast.

Duncan lifted a hand, slowing the riders near a narrow aperture in the woods. The grass grew long and ripe, ideal grazing for Highland deer.

"Take the horses back the way we came. Hobble them on the road, then we should hide near the clearing, weapons at the ready. This appears to be a popular spot for deer to feed."

The men reigned their horses around, and after tethering them on several low branches, they crept through the brush and settled in to wait for their quarry.

Duncan was correct. Shortly after they squatted in their places, an elegant red doe entered the blind, nipping at the ripe grasses. Rafe stiffened, fidgeting with his bow to take aim. In a silent move, Kellan lay his hand on Rafe's arm to still him. One eyebrow rose on Rafe's forehead. What were they doing, waiting? Why wait for a stag when the doe was here, a perfect shot?

His question was answered a heartbeat later. A magnificent beast stepped out of the thicket and joined the red doe. His branched antlers reached higher than even mighty Duncan, with knife-tips for points. The creature's burnished fur paled as it crossed his chest. It lifted its nose, sniffing the blind, and Rafe had no doubt the red stag was convinced of their presence. He was not enticed by the tender grass as the doe was. Instead, he remained on alert.

'Twould be a tremendous challenge to take him down. No wonder the clan waited on the doe.

The arrow struck the stag's chest before Rafe heard the bushes rustle. The arrow held true, and the stag leapt up in protest, emitting a bellow that sent the doe running. A flurry of other arrows completed the hard task, and once the stag was downed, the men left the brush to collect their spoils. Rafe held back, letting the Fraser men work, securing their prize.

So focused on the prospect of fresh meat for their supper, the Fraser men didn't hear another rustling in the bushes on the far side of the clearing. Rafe lifted his head, straining to listen and confirm that he had indeed heard something. He wasn't sure he heard anything.

Nothing but the celebratory noise of the Frasers. Brenna had squeezed her tiny frame between several men, trying to take part on preparing the stag. The larger men, however, had pushed Brenna aside. She was standing just outside the cluster of men when the rustling sound attracted Rafe's attention again. He lay a cautious hand on the dirk in his waistband and pulled his broadsword from its sheath in a silent move.

The next scene unfolded in a frenzied blur, and Rafe wasn't certain of what he was seeing until his body reacted. The explosion of snarling from the bush made the men jump, scrambling for their swords.

The boar moved with alarming speed, and snapped around, the tusks ripping past Nevan as it roared toward Brenna in a flash.

Her dirk was in her hand, but Rafe knew 'twas a weak weapon against the boar's bristly hide. She'd be lucky if she even managed to scratch it with the blade. Kellan leapt toward the boar. From his distance, though, the beast would be on Brenna before he'd be close enough to bring his sword down.

All these thoughts flashed through Rafe's mind as his body moved without thinking. It was a pure instinct to the threat, a warrior's immediate reaction to the boar.

In two quick strides, Rafe inserted himself between Brenna and the oncoming wild pig. Her eyes were wide with fear, an absolute, paralyzing fear. She'd managed to keep a hold on her dirk, but then froze, unable to move against the menace of the bellowing beast.

The men in the wood stilled, watching the horrendous event unfold before their eyes. The air and sounds of the grove were silent, waiting, everything focused on the boar bearing down on Rafe and the diminutive Brenna shielded behind him. Clutching her knife to her chest, she stared at Rafe in shocked horror — he was prepared to take on the full brunt of the beast.

Rafe's body was perfectly positioned. He gripped the pommel of his sword in a battle stance, ready to thrust the broadsword when the boar was at just the right position. Too far, and he'd do naught but nick the hardened skin and the boar would be on them both. Too late, and well, it'd be too late. The rough hooves and sharp, knife-like tusks would tear at their flesh before he could thrust his sword at the beast.

The pig snarled again as it approached Rafe. Brenna could have reached out and touched its dripping snout.

Then in a formidable sweep, Rafe brought his sword down in a fierce arc, slicing the boar's skin exactly where it needed to — in the softer spot of the boar's neck, right above the shoulder. The blade slipped in with a crunch, and the boar squealed before dropping to the dirt. It heaved once and shuddered, its blood pooling out.

Rafe remained poised with his sword above the boar, watching for it to move again. The entire crowd exhaled, breathing again after the harrowing few seconds that had transpired. Brenna crumpled into Rafe, supporting herself against his backside. Whipping around, he caught her before she collapsed completely.

"Bren! Are ye injured?"

Kellan and Duncan pushed Rafe aside, turning Brenna over to search for a wound. Panic sat thick in Rafe's throat. Had he missed the beast? Had the boar caught Brenna as it burst from the underbrush?

Finding nothing, Kellan patted at Brenna's cheeks, trying to rouse her. She blinked in quick succession, opening her eyes to a collection of worried faces hovering above her. She pushed herself upright. Kellan placed a shaky grip on her shoulder.

"Bren, are ye well? Did the boar injure ye?" he queried, his face tight with worry.

Brenna shook her head.

"Nay. I think 'twas terror and seeing Rafe stab the boar." She realized his chiseled face was missing amongst those surrounding her. "Rafe!"

"Here, Bren," he answered from behind her.

Brenna twisted around to see him. Apparently uninjured, he crouched a few paces back, wiping his stained blade in the grass to clean it.

"Are ye injured?"

"Nay," he answered in a casual tone, as though he fought off boars daily.

Duncan's eyes focused on Brenna when he spoke to Rafe.

"MacLeod, thank ye for your quick actions."

Kellan and the rest of the men were catering to Brenna, readying themselves, the stag, and the boar to return to the keep. Rafe continued to wipe at his blade. He didn't respond to Duncan.

"MacLeod?" Duncan asked again, raising a bushy blond eyebrow. "MacLeod, are ye hearing me?"

Rafe's head snapped up, a reddened shadow high on his cheeks.

"Aye, I hear ye, man."

Duncan lifted his other eyebrow in suspicion. "Woolgathering again?"

Rafe shifted his attention back to his sword, which was as clean as he was going to get it in the grass.

"Aye. A character flaw, I admit."

"I wanted to thank ye for your quick actions on behalf of Bren."

Rafe shrugged and slid his broadsword into the scabbard on his back.

"'Twas no more than anyone would have done. I happened to be close enough to Bren to step in."

A sharp slap landed on Rafe's shoulder.

"And 'tis a good thing ye did! Venison and boar in the larder! We have a lot of work ahead of us, but then a feast as a reward!" Nevan cheered.

Nevan's excitement over the surprise bounty was infectious. Rafe's own smile joined those of the other men.

The only one immune to Nevan's enthusiasm was Duncan. He strode to his horse and mounted, but the unyielding lines of his face remained fixated on one person.

And it wasn't Brenna.

***

Dorcas's words echoed in Brenna's head as they rode back to the keep. Her words, the conversation with her uncle, and her own heightened emotions, all roiled and rose to a pitch inside her. If kissing Rafe was Dorcas's recommendation for getting to know the man better, what sort of reward had he earned in saving her life?

Because that is truly what the man had done. While she'd held her dirk in her hand, ready to strike at the boar, any warrior worthy of the name knew that a paltry knife in her slender hand, no matter how well forged the blade, was no weapon against a wild boar.

Then, before she could lift her arm in defense, Rafe was there, his body a shield against the danger. He put his life in peril for her, to save her, and he'd only just met her. He wasn't a Fraser, wasn't tasked with guarding her, yet there he had been, sword in hand.

And with bulging muscles and one mighty swing, he struck the beast down.

He did it for her.

Dorcas was right. At the very least, the man was deserving of a kiss.

That thought brought on a whole new slew of concerns. What if he outright rejected her? She'd seen him kiss Dawn, and he had received her kiss well. Brenna glanced at her clothing — she wasn't exactly dressed in womanly skirts. She still had boar blood on her tunic. Might he want a kiss from a blood-covered, braies-wearing woman?

There was only one way to find out.

After settling the horses with the stable lads, Brenna stepped past the stable doors, awaiting Rafe's exit. She needed to time it correctly, otherwise Nevan or Kellan would follow her, and that was not what she wanted.

If this were to be her first kiss, she wanted to be as ready as possible. Her heart pounded in her chest as Rafe rounded the doorway.

"Rafe, if ye please? Might I have a word?" Her voice was high-pitched and shaky. Rafe came to her side.

He, too, still wore the remnants of the day. Coated in a film of dirt, sweat, and wild boar blood, his raven hair in unruly disarray, he appeared the fierce Highland warrior in full. Her heart thrummed at the magnificent sight of him.

"What do ye need, Bren?" he asked, approaching her in a long stride.

"Brenna. Ye can call me Brenna. I think I shall start dropping the Bren nickname. 'Twas fitting when I was a child, but no' anymore, and most only use it when we are around strangers."

"Aye," Rafe agreed. "Ye would struggle to pass as a bairn or a lad. Brenna suits ye."

Every word from him made her heart take flight. She swallowed the tight nervousness in her throat.

"I wanted to thank ye for today. Ye were brave, stepping in front of the boar as ye did. Ye may have well saved my life."

Rafe's discomfort with her accolades brought a light pink shade to his cheeks. She imagined she could even see it under the scruff of his midnight-hued beard of his jawline. A modicum of confidence blossomed in her chest.

"I did nothing any other man would have. I just happened to be closest to ye —"

"Aye, but ye still did it." Gathering her courage, Brenna took another step toward Rafe, closing the distance between them until their tunics touched. "I thank ye. I think ye deserve —"

"Bren!"

The sharp, angry shout from Kellan surprised them both, causing Bren and Rafe to jump apart as though they had been caught doing something wrong.

And while they hadn't, Brenna almost had. She rubbed her hand over her cropped hair, trying to cover her actions.

"What are ye doing over here, Bren?" Kellan asked her, but his suspicious eyes didn't leave Rafe. Kellan watched him like a falcon.

"Kel, I wished to thank the man for saving me —" Brenna started, but Kellan yanked her arm, dragging her away from Rafe. He moved to follow, to halt Kellan, then thought better of it.

"I think ye thanked him enough," Kellan told her. "Come, ye are needed in the keep. Your uncle will want to see how ye fare after today, as will your da."

Mentioning her father was a lousy trick, but it worked. Casting a quick glance over her shoulder, Brenna captured Rafe's gaze, holding it for several heartbeats before stumbling after Kellan.

A mix of irritation and frustration churned inside her.

So much for my first kiss.

***

Frustrated over the news of Brenna's near-miss with the boar, Robert coveted time with his brother to soothe his annoyances. And when his struggles or irritations were at their height, a visit with his brother, and his nurse Anne, was enough to calm his inner turmoil. He craved these meetings for his own selfish reasons as much as he made the visits for Kevin's benefit.

The door to Kevin's chamber was closed, as was required by Robert, and locked. The last time they'd left the door ajar, Kevin had managed to sneak past the sleeping maid and make his way into the yard, wearing nothing but a stained shift. Nevan and Kellan had found the Laird stumbling around the stables, looking for something he believed he had lost.

The Laird hadn't lost anything in the stables – he hadn't been there in months. Nevan understood the Laird's confusion led to strange encounters and escorted the complaining man back to his room before anyone saw him.

The clan had been struggling under the weight of a sickly Laird until Robert assumed control, but if they well knew the level of Kevin's incapacitation, 'twould further devastate an already devastated people. Robert had worked with his closest men to keep the true depth of the Laird's illness hidden.

Robert knocked at the door, and the tall house maid answered. Since Anne had been selected specifically for this task, she spent most of her time with the Laird in his rooms. Robert had a deep appreciation for the remarkable amount of patience she'd shown with Kevin when his memory and behavior slid to a new low. Anne used a tender hand to feed and bathe him, to answer his many, many questions, and to speak to him in a tone that helped him stay calm. Robert saw her as a saint on earth and gave up a prayer of thankfulness for her presence nightly.

Her long, dark hair was bound back in a simple kerchief, and a candle with the scents of lavender and heather burned in the corner of the room. "It helps soothe him," she'd told Robert when she requested more. "The memories he talks of when they burn are good ones."

Shortly after the death of Maud, they had learned the difference between those good and bad memories when he'd tried to take a broadsword to Robert, thinking him a MacKay coming to abduct Brenna. It had taken four men to disarm him and get him back to bed.

'Twas Anne who shooed them away and brought out the candle, then placed a cool cloth on Kevin's head and hummed a child's lullaby until his fretful state left.

Robert saw Anne with new eyes that day. 'Twas the moment Anne had become Robert's favorite person. Their romance began not long after.

"How's my brother today?"

'Twas the question they had to ask before they could see him. If 'twas a bad day, then Anne might recommend he return later. Today was not that day. Anne's bright eyes sparkled when she rested them on Robert's face.

"Today is a good day, milord. Welcome. He will be pleased to see ye, I think."

Robert took her hand and gave it a subtle squeeze, then walked with heavy feet to the bed where his beloved brother was wasting away, both in body and in mind. His watery green eyes lit up under heavy lids at the sight of Robert.

"Robbie! 'Tis so good ye are here! Are ye to join me for supper?"

Robert flicked his gaze to Anne, who shrugged.

"Uh, nay, Kevin. 'Tis closer to midday. But if ye are hungry, I'll gladly share a meal with ye."

Kevin gave Robert a toothy grin that wrenched Robert's heart; his brother seemed too old and so young at the same time. And to be called Robbie, his childhood nickname, made that dichotomy worse.

"We have your favorite, Robbie. Oats and honey!"

"Aye, 'tis my favorite," Robert agreed. He hadn't loved oats and honey so much since he was a child. Kevin had lost years again.

"And will that pretty lassie join ye? I'll have Maud join us."

Robert blinked back tears. He probably cried more than any Highland man should, but to see his powerful big brother laid so low, to hear him speak of his wife as though she were still alive, was heart wrenching.

What had started as forgetfulness and odd quirks had deteriorated into a sickness of the mind that robbed Kevin of the powerful man he used to be. The man who led the clan with pride and determination, the man who wooed and won the beautiful Maud's hand, that man was now a shadow of his former self.

Too soon, Robert and his men must push Kevin's laird ship aside, and Robert would step up to assume the chieftainship in its entirety. And that day was on the horizon. Duncan and Nevan had already been in discussions with Robert about it.

The need was great. The sooner Robert assumed leadership, the better their clan would be. But taking that step was akin to putting the final stone on his brother's funeral cairn. And everything they had been through in the past six years would be pushed into history. Braden, Maud, even poor Brenna-turned-Bren.

Brenna. Was she prepared for Robert to set her father aside and take control? Little by little, she had been regaining herself, coming out of her shell. Robert's head pounded as he smiled at his brother, the weight of these thoughts threatening to split his head in two.

There was no good answer, but Brenna's recent changes in her behavior just might lessen the impact. She would have to see how poorly her father's health was and prepare for yet another shift in her clan.

Kevin finished his oats and drifted off as Robert watched. He prayed Brenna handled the change with grace and peace instead of with fear and sadness.

She'd had enough of the latter to last three lifetimes.

Chapter Seven: The Arc of Change

BRENNA COULDN'T DENY the rising passions she'd had for Rafe since he rescued her in the wood. Nay, even before that, since they'd first met. They had a strong connection, that Brenna could not deny, something new and curious she'd not felt before. The moments they shared were magic, at least for Brenna. And Rafe seemed to enjoy it, if the intensity in his face was any indication.

For the past several days, whenever his eyes caught her gaze, her heart fluttered. He didn't seem to care if she wore braies or a kirtle. And he conversed with her openly and honestly, not with a stifling fear of her fragility, which was how everyone else spoke to her — as if one wrong word would break her again.

They'd shared several private conversations since the hunt, out of view of her lax guards, each one more intimate than the last. And he wasn't overeager to resume his travels to the Bruce, which pleased Brenna immensely. He hadn't asked about the returning Frasers or commented on leaving. She hesitated to admit it, but she longed for the man to stay.

One cloudy afternoon, she found Rafe mucking out the barn and brought him a midday meal of boiled venison and black bread. He took it with a grateful smile and walked the short distance to the gardens, then sat with her on the stone wall behind the barn. His involvement in her and her clan grew with each meeting, and Brenna marveled at the ease they found in each other's company.

Spending time with Rafe helped her feel the most comfortable in her own skin. She didn't feel she had to hide when she was with him; she could be whoever she felt like being.

Today, their light conversation became deeper as he learned more about her.

When she mentioned her limited contact with anyone outside her clan ("drinks at an inn notwithstanding," she'd told him in a sardonic tone), his eyebrows spiked high on his forehead.

Rafe had not heard of such a thing for a chieftain's lass. From his experience, grown women, especially those who are the daughters of powerful lairds, were handfast well before their 18th year. Had she hid so much that no suitor expressed an interest? Aye, her father was ill, but had her uncle been neglectful in that duty?

Moreover, how could a man look at Brenna, braies and bonnet or no, and *not* see the stunning woman under the costume?

"Do ye plan on marriage?" he asked. "Does your father, or your uncle, want ye to wed? As the daughter of a laird and all . . ."

'Twas an odd, unexpected question, but had any part of her life followed the norms of the Highlands? Brenna shook her short, coppery hair.

"Aye. No' only 'tis expected of me, but I also want to be wed. I've hidden from the world for so long. Even though I put on the mantel of a lad, I don't want to be one. I would hope to have a husband, someone who loves and stands as a guard against the world for me. I'd like bairns. But I've hidden for years, 'tis comfortable for me. 'Tis a bit of a conflict, aye?"

Rafe remained quiet, watching the mist move across the glen. Though the air was warm for high summer, the damp mist clung and clung. A gentle movement to his left caught his attention, and he pointed at a butterfly, which was little more than a glint of orange in the mist above the thistles.

"I think ye are no' unlike that butterfly. Ye know what a butterfly is? How it starts its life?"

Brenna tipped her head to catch a glimpse of orange and black wings.

"Aye," she answered. "Every bairn kens that caterpillars form a wrap around themselves, then emerge as beautifully vibrant butterflies in the late spring."

Rafe kept his face focused on the dainty, winged beauty.

92

"Aye. But they dinna leave that hard outer shell until they are ready. Otherwise, their wings aren't formed, and they canna fly."

Rafe turned his face to Brenna, who still watched the erratic wings of the butterfly with rapt attention. The delicate lines of her profile were as fetching as the butterfly she admired.

"I think ye are like that," he continued. "Ye, as a child, sad and afraid, a frail, wingless caterpillar. Then, ye wrapped yourself in your brother's clothes, in his plaid *breacan*."

Brenna sat up tall on the log and looked at Rafe, the intensity in her eyes burning through him, her body clenching at his words. Her brow furrowed at him as she waited for him to continue.

"Once the time is right, ye will shed that clothing, and ye will show the world what a beauty ye are. And all the world will marvel at ye. But not before your time."

Rafe lifted her plaid from where she draped it on the wall and wrapped it protectively around her shoulders, like a caterpillar in its cocoon.

"Right now, this is your outer shell. And when ye are ready, ye will fly. But not yet," he said, fastening the large plaid playfully so her whole body was hidden beneath it. His eyes were soft with understanding. "But not yet."

***

Their conversation waned as they cleared the remnants of the meal and resumed their work. They had neared the barn when Rafe's question of marriage returned to her mind.

"From what I can guess of your presence here on Fraser land, ye dinna have a lass at home?" she asked him. If he did, yet spent his time at the Frasers kissing women, Brenna's estimation of him would shift in a heartbeat. She might not want to get to know him better if that were the case. She'd just assumed . . .

She breathed an invisible sigh of relief when he shook his head.

"Nay. I loitered with some rough men of my clan and never took life with the seriousness that a true man should. 'Twould have been unfair to thrust that upon a lass in marriage. 'Twas only when I decided to leave that I realized I needed to improve myself and be a man, not a worthless *leadaí*."

Rafe paused, flicking his cerulean gaze at her. No time like the present to let the lass know his own intentions — what he had of them. "'Twas another reason. First, I had to become a better man, then I had to find a woman who appealed to me. The new man. There is something to be said for venturing out into the world and finding someone different, one who does no' know of your past."

A deep rosy blush stained Brenna's cheeks. Was he talking about her? She preferred to think so, but suspected 'twas nothing more than a girlish fancy and put that thought from her mind.

"While I do want to wed, I think I fear the prospect," she admitted, since they were sharing secrets. "At least a bit. 'Tis a reason why I still hide. This life, 'tis all I have known. What if I

94

canna play the role of wife well? I have no' even kissed a man afore."

"No man in your clan has offered for ye at all? That I canna believe."

A sour expression crossed Brenna's dainty features, and her nose crinkled. "Nay. No' a one. Who wants a woman who wears men's clothing? They think I'm touched in the head. And who wants the daughter of an ill man? They dinna even ken how sick he is. Who knows what they think of him."

"Touched in the head?" One thick black eyebrow rose on Rafe's head. Other than her odd dress and sometimes boyish hobbies, she'd seemed of sound mind.

That sour look sunk into her features even more.

"Surely, if they see what a fine-looking lass ye are outside of your brother's clothes —" he tried to explain.

"Ye think me fine-looking?"

Her wide, innocent eyes overwhelmed her entire face. *Nay*, he told himself. She was more. Stunning, radiant. Those were the words he should have said to her.

A pang of sadness thrust through Rafe. Such a harrowing childhood, the loss of so much, and then to be almost punished for wanting to hide from the cruelties of the world was so unfair. Had no one ever told her how comely she was? No wonder she remained in her brother's clothes.

Again, Rafe wanted to be as honest as he could within the parameters of his great lie. He reached a strong hand across the short distance between them, brushing at a loose tendril that framed her face.

"Aye. I dinna think ye can pass for a man much longer."

The heady tone of his voice matched his words. She was a stunning woman, and Rafe was shocked no one else saw it.

***

His words made Brenna's heart flutter under her breast in an unfamiliar thrill of anxiety and excitement. For so long, people overlooked her. Now, here was a man, a full Highland warrior, and those sky-blue eyes burned past her skin to her center.

She wanted to drop her eyes, to look away, yet she didn't. She couldn't. For the first time in her life, someone was gazing at her — at Brenna. Not as a bairn, not as a lad. A man was capturing her gaze, his eyes melting into hers with forceful intensity. Her chest quivered the longer their shared look lasted.

So focused as she was on his heated gaze that never wavered, that she didn't notice he leaned into her. Or had she leaned closer to him?

Brenna didn't know. But his gaze on her was mightier than a lodestone, drawing them together until his lips were a breath from hers.

Then she lifted on her toes and closed the gap, pressing her chaste lips on his, feeling the light sensation as his lips worked against hers, the tickle of his facial hair against her skin. And the heat. Oh, the heat! The burning that kindled between their lips and lapped over her in waves.

Is this what love was? Her thoughts ran in a rampant frenzy as the kiss lingered, a mix of light touching and deeper movement, of the parting of lips and his tongue on hers in a fiery shock. Is this what she had missed while hiding as a lad? Was this what she wanted?

And as her mouth moved without her guidance, stroking his tongue in return, her whole body screamed *aye*.

Aye, this was what she wanted.

Then another question on the tail of that thought. Why hadn't she wanted it before? But she knew the answer to that question before it even appeared in her mind.

She wanted Rafe. That was the difference.

He snapped his head back in a sudden move, his face reddened from their exertions. He stepped away quickly, adjusting the plaid around his hips.

"Nay, lass. Ye dinna want me," he breathed in a ragged voice, seeming to read her mind.

Her face was congested with shock, her dismayed eyes wide. Her offended expression cut him to the core, and he softened his gaze. He hadn't meant to push her away with such ferocity.

"I think ye are more than ready to be a wife," he told her in a gentle tone.

Then he held his arm out, gesturing her to enter the yard before him. After surveying Rafe over his strange shift in behavior,

Brenna, resuming her character of Bren, held her head high and entered the yard.

In that moment, she transformed into her shadow self, hiding that passion he'd just experienced under a shabby tunic.

She might be able to fool her clan, her guards, her uncle, but Brenna had an idea that she was not fooling Rafe. He saw her beneath her clothes, beneath her disguise.

And that thought sent a surge of quivering excitement coursing through her. She didn't care what he claimed or how he protested. She did want him.

***

Searching around the yard to make sure none of Brenna's guards watched with angry glares, Rafe returned to his work in the barn, his mind spinning.

He was fortunate Duncan or his men hadn't seen that kiss, because if they had, they would have recognized the passion behind it, and Rafe would be lucky to leave the Fraser clan with his life.

What had he done?

Grabbing the pitchfork, he then shoveled old hay and animal droppings with a vengeance, trying to wear out the lust that peaked inside him with a fury.

His conscience, slow as it was, must have got the better of him. Any affections the lass had for him were for a man she didn't know. A man who was lying to her. He had led her on. That's what he had done.

Had he meant to? Was that his intention? Rafe shook his head, his ebony locks swaying around his head. Nay. He had wanted a friend, a feeling of community from the Frasers.

What happened with Brenna took on a life of its own. The minute he saw her as she truly was that day at the loch, 'twas as if a wick had been lit, a slow burning wick that led to a puddle of vitriol. The more time he spent with her, the further that wick burned. And that kiss — the flame reached the oil and burst into an uncontrollable fire.

He hadn't been able to control himself. 'Twas all he could do not to crush her to him, cover her lips out of pure, animalistic hunger. She had looked so rejected when he thrust her away, and he wanted to gather her into his arms and tell her everything — tell her who he was, admit his own desire for her, confess she affected him in a way he didn't believe possible.

Every ounce of will power. He would need every bit to stop his inflamed longing. He tried to hide it, but he was shaking when he stepped back. Shaking with that virulent yearning for her.

As much as he wanted her, craved her, burned for her, he was a stranger to her.

Brenna needed to find herself, take her place in her clan, and find a man, a Fraser would be best, to marry and continue her family line.

The hay flew harder as he worked his frustrations out in the barn.

The last thing she needed was a lying scoundrel like Rafe. He had to keep his distance.

***

Once she was certain Rafe had departed and could no longer see her, Brenna charged into the tower in a flurry of over-sized plaid and raced up the narrow stone steps to her chambers — her brother's chambers. In a huff, she threw herself on her simple bed and lay her hand over her heart.

While she had tried to put on an austere mask in front of her clan, her chest hadn't ceased throbbing since Rafe's fervent eyes shifted into that heated gaze and rocked her to her core. And his lips on hers! 'Twas nothing short of amazing.

How had one man, a dark stranger, managed to take everything she knew in the world and turn it on its head?

She let her eyes glance around the room as her thoughts remained on the wickedly handsome Rafe and his bold kiss. He could see beyond the mask she wore and see the woman beneath, and she didn't know if she should be pleased or worried.

Pleased, her mind told her.

That mask extended to her room. Other lasses, even those living with large families in tiny crofts, had a more feminine living space than she did. The room had been Braden's, and the character of the former occupant was still heavily stamped within its walls.

A rough-hewn table was shoved against the wall near the cold hearth and was home to a broken tooth antler comb. With her shorter hair and tendency to sport a woolly Scots bonnet, nary a ribbon broke the stark gray and brown of the room.

Several of her brother's dirks, a collection which she hadn't dared touch, were displayed in a thin layer of dust on a shelf. Her brother's trunk that she pilfered through on a regular basis sat beneath.

Even the bedding under her was a rag-tag assortment of cast-off plaids and a few furs, no neat coverlet or new tartan.

Not that none had been offered. Over the years, her beloved uncle had encouraged her to come out of her shell, promising her that her father was well past the time of needing a replacement son (*well past the time of recalling he even had a child,* Brenna thought bitterly). He'd explained that the clan understood why she'd dressed in her brother's tunics and kilts for so long, and they would also understand when she decided to resume her role as the lady of the keep in her mother's stead.

But she'd been daunted at the prospect of so much responsibility, of changing how she'd lived for years. And as Rafe had said, she wasn't ready. Not yet.

Brenna shoved herself into a sitting position, her feet dangling off the bed. Mayhap she did need more time, but she could start preparing herself, right? She could start that transformation. Butterflies didn't burst from their cocoons all at once. Neither did baby chicks from their eggs! 'Twas a slow process, the transition from the known inside the shell to the new world outside.

Mayhap 'tis what she needed. To start the transition. A beginning.

Rafe's words and his surprising kiss — that was the crack in her shell. After all these years, perchance 'twas time to get ready.

101

But where to start? She recalled little of skirts and ribbons she may have worn as a child. She had vague memories of her mother brushing her hair and tying the side back with ribbon. To do the same to her own hair? Brenna didn't know where to begin. And flowers in her room, proper combs, sewing, gowns?

Other lasses had years to accumulate such feminine wealth. They had mothers to help them. Years and a mother she'd lost.

She would require help. A lot of help.

Brenna leapt off the bed and rushed the door, emitting a low shriek when she opened it as Dawn stood right before her, a wooden platter precariously balanced in one hand as she tried to knock.

"Oh, my dear Bren! I did no' mean to give ye such a fright!"

"Nay, Dawn, I was caught up in my own thoughts and was no' paying attention. Please, do enter."

Dawn swept into the room, and Brenna watched as the kitchen maid seemed to glide as she walked. Dawn placed the platter of cheese and eggs on the table and swung back around, stopping short as Brenna waited next to her, scrutinizing her with a strange intensity.

"Do ye need something? Have I forgotten —?"

Brenna waved her hand at Dawn and laughed with a shaky voice.

"Nay, I was just . . . that is to say . . ."

Dawn waited patiently as Brenna searched to find the right words.

"'Tis been a long while since I wore skirts," Brenna said.

One slender blonde eyebrow rose on Dawn's forehead as a knowing look settled into her features. "Aye?"

"I've worn my brother's clothes for nigh six years. All of my maturity."

Dawn's other eyebrow joined its match.

"Aye?"

"'Tis to say, would it be strange —? Do ye think—?"

"Do ye want to dress as a lass again?" Dawn asked in an excited rush, clapping her hands under her chin.

A look of absolute horror contorted Brenna's features, and Dawn erupted into a fit of giggles.

"Ooch, no' so far as that? Then what can I help ye with?"

"I'm no' ready," Brenna admitted. "No' yet. But 'tis time to prepare. My father will no' longer know or care if I dress as my brother or myself. My sadness over my brother and mother is, well, still present, but more of a deep bruise on my heart than a gaping wound. I've hidden from the world, from my clan, from my kin for years. I must shed that mantle, but I need time."

A slip of a smile tugged at Dawn's gentle lips. "Is that the only reason for ye to want to come out of your shell?" she hinted.

Brenna didn't raise her eyes, a touch of awkwardness keeping her silent.

"I knew it! I did! The handsome raven-haired MacLeod with eyes like the loch in the morn?"

"Dawn!" Brenna slapped her hands across her worn tunic. Dawn's eyes followed them, roving over the tattered remains of the clothing.

"So, no skirts, not yet. What would ye have me do?"

Brenna's eyes cast around the chambers, and Dawn noted her glance.

"Your room?"

"If I'm going to dress, to resume my place as a lady of the clan, daughter of the Laird, I canna think it to happen overnight. Even my room is that of a man's. I have no dresses, combs, ribbons, water bowl, nothing. If we can start in my chambers, then perchance find some kirtles and gowns that may fit?"

Dawn studied the short-haired lass who, for so long, hid from her own destiny. Dawn had adored the Lady Fraser, pined like every other lass in the clan for Brenna's charming brother Braden, and was devoted to her laird. And though she too had found the mysterious MacLeod Highlander an exotic distraction, 'twas all the man was for Dawn: a distraction.

Her lady, hiding away out of fear and loneliness, now needed her. And Dawn was the woman who could help Brenna finally break free from her past.

Chapter Eight: Painted Discoveries

"COME."

Dawn grabbed Brenna's hand and dragged her from her chambers. They scurried down the hall to the room at the end. Tucked beneath the shadows and cobwebs was the door to Maud's room.

"Nay! I canna!" Brenna screeched. To come face to face with the ghost of her mother? What was Dawn thinking?

"Ye can and ye will!" Dawn urged her. "If ye can live in your brother's old chambers these years past, ye can now visit your mother's room. In truth, someone should have done this for ye long ago."

The creaking door shifted in a cloud of dust as Dawn pushed it open. And Brenna's eyes rested on her mother's belongings for the first time in years.

Dawn stepped back, waiting for Brenna to take the lead and enter. Brenna blinked into the dust for several moments, then with a shaky breath, she set foot in her mother's chambers.

Naught had changed in six years. 'Twas as if time stopped in this room the day her mother passed into the arms of the angels. Dust motes floated in the stale air of the room.

Truthfully, she was surprised her uncle hadn't had the room cleared out once her father had slipped further into his condition. The space could have use for something else, rather than as a shrine to a dead woman.

Most striking was a portrait, a canvas too breathtaking to be hidden away in a remote Scots tower, hung in a plain frame over the hearth. Her mother's face shone from the canvas in a pale relief, accented with touches of blues and greens in the shoulders of the gown. 'Twasn't a large painting, but in a world where such beauty usually resided in churches and cathedrals, to see such an image in her mother's room filled Brenna with astonishment. How had she not known of this picture or recalled it in her memories? Had she blocked that memory with so many others?

Brenna approached the painting with fascination, enthralled with her mother's depiction, a woman she hadn't seen in six years. Tears collected against her lashes and fell in warm droplets to her cheeks. But Brenna didn't notice. She reached up to touch the portrait with a hesitant finger, as though she were touching her mother herself. Her mind reeled, and she wished a similar painting of her brother existed so she could see him once again.

An image like this one was pricey — few outside the realm of kings and churches owned such artistry. Where had it come from?

"Do ye ken how she came to have this?" Brenna asked Dawn.

She asked the question without turning around, unable to tear her gaze from the soft curves of Maud's face. Her chest ached, not only the pain of a child missing her mother, but anger of what she'd been robbed.

"I did it," a deep voice boomed from the doorway, and Brenna swirled around to find her uncle leaning against the chamber door. Dawn was tucked to the side, trying not to interfere. Brenna's eyes flicked from Dawn's encouraging smile to Robert.

His face, his entire stance, reflected the same mix of sadness and anger that Brenna felt. Too often 'twas easy to forget her uncle lost his family, too. Plus, the man had the weight of the clan on his shoulders, making his burden even heavier to bear.

Robert's gaze was riveted on the painting of Maud, his eyes shining with his own tears as he looked up at the gentle beauty so many years gone.

"I had it commissioned before she wed your father. A painter, a young man trying to make a name for himself in hopes of obtaining a commission from a nobleman or the church." Robert's voice took on a lighter tone, so different from his typical thick growl.

"The lad was a skinny man with a stand and some pigments in the village. Your father and I were there with Maud, and I approached the man, asked if he could paint from memory. I told him, if he could, an extra groat would find its way into his palm. He agreed, and I walked Kevin and Maud past the lad a few times, coming up with the worst excuses for why we had to walk from one end of the market again and again."

The tears in his eyes stained his cheeks above the shadow of a smile that the remembrance brought to his lips. Brenna's heart wrenched at her uncle's forlorn expression of heartache and joy.

"She looked so comely that day. Her gown was the color of the sky on a late spring day, her plaid draped over her shoulder in case it grew cold. Her hair, a bronzed color of newly hewn metals was loose, as she hadn't yet wed Kevin. I stupidly hoped that, if I presented her this painting as a gift, she might choose me over my brother. A young man's foolish hope," he added, shrugging to no one in particular.

Then he caught himself, shaking his head and wiping the tears from his cheeks with the palm of his hand. The love, the tension in his voice spoke louder than his flowery words. His eyes finally moved from the painting of Maud that dominated the room to Brenna. His smile faltered.

"She was full with your brother, though no one kent it. She wed my brother a month later, took up the mantle of Lady of the keep with ease, and delivered a healthy baby boy before the following spring. I'd never seen my brother so happy. I couldn't tread on his joy. I gave them the painting as a wedding gift."

Brenna felt her uncle's pain in her own heart. She'd known he was close to both her mother and father; she'd just not known how close. Or why he never wed and had bairns of his own. Why he permitted this room to remain untouched after so many years.

"Oh, Uncle," was all she could think of to say.

"Ye are so like her. Do ye see it?"

Brenna could see her hair, her eyes, even her round cheeks in her mother's portrait. She nodded. Robert cleared his throat.

"Why are ye here, Brenna? I came up to see if ye were going to visit your father and saw the door ajar."

"Is it wrong for me to be here? Do ye want me to leave?"

Robert shook his head, stepping into the room. "Of course, ye can be here. 'Tis your mother's room. But 'tis the first time I've known ye to come here."

Brenna's eyes flitted nervously from her uncle to the image above the hearth.

"Do ye think—?" she started, then paused, looking over her tattered clothes. "I've lived like this for so long. Do ye think she's disappointed in me? For hiding as I did?"

The strain in her voice would have caused the most hardened warrior to weep. Robert rushed his niece, enclosing her slender form in a rough hug.

They stood in the middle of the room crying together, under the kind, painted eyes of Maud. Their tears of loss and pain whetted them, washing them like rain from the heavens washes the earth.

Dawn stepped out of the room to wait in the hall, not wanting to intrude more than she already had.

***

Robert regained control of his emotions first and put Brenna at arm's length. Then he bent low so his earthy brown eyes held hers.

"Know this, Brenna. Your good mother has spent the past six years looking down on ye with pride and for protection. She kens how much ye hurt after your brother passed, she hurt, too. So much that it killed her. I ken she knows living in your brother's clothes, in your brother's life, was a way to heal your heart."

"Ye dinna think 'twas wrong?"

Robert released her and stood at his full height, considering.

"Who's to say? I gave up on love and bairns out of love for your mother. Your mother's heartache led to her death after your brother died, and your father's illness worsened. Who is to say what is right or wrong when we cope with grief? Not I. If ye needed to live in Braden's room, sleep in his bed, and wear his clothes as a way to grapple with your loss, I canna say 'tis wrong. Only someone who has walked that harrowing path can say, and I dinna ken anyone who has walked a stonier path than ye, lassie."

Brenna took her uncle's words to heart and his calloused hand in her own.

"Or ye, Uncle."

Robert cleared his throat again, tamping down the cloying sentiments that threatened to spill over once more.

"So, lassie. Why are ye here?"

"I heard a good piece of advice today, Uncle. That MacLeod man, he noted that I may not be ready yet, but I can get ready, for when I no longer wished to hide away out of pain and heartache. But I dinna ken how to do that. I've worn braies and tunics and short hair for so long. How do I make that change? Dawn recommended I begin here."

Dawn reappeared in the doorway at the sound of her name. She gave the pair a tight smile, praying that she'd done the right thing.

"Dawn had the right of it," Robert agreed, bobbing his head at Dawn, who let loose a pent-up sigh of relief. "What do ye need to start? To get ye ready?"

Dawn stepped up, full of questions and advice.

"Do ye want to stay in your brother's chambers, Brenna, and make changes? Or would ye rather keep it as 'tis and move into a new room?"

A deep ache in her chest erupted at the prospect of leaving her brother's room. Panic filled Brenna's gaze, and her uncle interjected.

"We already have one shrine, Brenna. Methinks ye may do well to know ye are always in your brother's chambers, under his care, even if we change what is in that room."

Her uncle's advice was sage and comforting. Brenna's anxiety tempered as she turned to Dawn.

"Yes. I'd prefer to remain in my brother's chambers."

"Do ye want to take some of your mother's belongings, or furniture, into that room?" Robert offered, and surprise replaced the dread in Brenna's chest. A thrust of agony pierced Robert's own heart to make that offer, to plunder the shrine of Brenna's beloved mother.

But in that moment of silence, they knew a truth that no one wanted to speak. The dead didn't need dressing tables, gowns, or ribbons.

Brenna, however, did.

"Dawn, help Brenna with whatever she wants. I'll retrieve a few men to move the furniture she desires."

Robert had made it to the door when Dawn threw a recommendation over her shoulder.

"See if ye can find the MacLeod man to help. Put the man to work."

Her comment was said in a casual tone. Yet, Robert's pursed lips told her that he knew why she made the suggestion and despised it. He left in a hurry.

"What do I do now, Dawn? I dinna ken what a lass requires."

"Weel," Dawn said as she scanned the room, tapping at her pert mouth with a fingernail, "Let's start with simple items and move from there, aye? Look about the chambers. What does your mother have that ye dinna have right now?"

Brenna followed Dawn's direction, letting her eyes fall on the tiny aspects that made her mother's room unique. A stack of shell combs caught her eyes.

"The combs?"

Dawn snatched them from the dressing table and blew on them, sending dust flying. Wiping the combs against her skirts, Dawn pulled the slouchy bonnet off Brenna's lustrous, hidden locks and tossed it on the bed. With a deft hand, she pulled the sides of Brenna's hair to her crown and secured them with the combs. That one change was the start of an avalanche.

"What next?" Dawn asked, her eyes dancing. She wanted Brenna to find joy in this moment, the same she felt for this lass, so long lost and alone. "Do ye want the entire dressing table?"

Brenna studied the table, trying to envision her mother sitting here, pulling her own coppery locks up with the combs. Brushing her hair until it flowed in a bronze river down her back. Brenna tried to see herself sitting there and couldn't. *Not yet,* she told herself, but maybe soon.

"Aye. Aye, I do." Her voice held a twinge of excitement.

Dawn clapped her hands at Brenna's choice and squealed as she removed more of the items and, finding a long-handled basket near the foot of the bed, placed the combs and other vanity items within to keep them secure.

A beaming smile split Dawn's face. Her exuberance was infectious, and she looked back to Brenna, whose own insides caught Dawn's delight.

"What next?" Dawn asked again.

***

Robert had found Kellan in the kitchens and ordered him to gather two other men to help remove furniture from Maud's chambers. He didn't tell Kellen to find the MacLeod man. Rafe was still an outsider, and though he'd proved himself on the hunt and had been a hard worker around the keep, Robert couldn't extend that much trust to the man. Duncan's comments regarding the MacLeod to Robert didn't sit well. Permitting his niece to engage with him overmuch was not, in Robert's estimation, sound thinking.

Duncan, Kellan, and Nevan had their commands to keep watch over his niece — and Robert had to hope that they were keeping the MacLeod from Brenna. Far from Brenna. She had enough to concern her without any added complications that the MacLeod might bring.

Several hulking Fraser warriors crowded in Maud's chambers as Dawn directed housemaids to begin a full scrubbing of "Bren's" rooms. The girls curtsied and raced to clean as quickly as possible before the new furniture was removed down the hall.

The old table and bed were taken out to make room for new bedding and her mother's dressing table. When they tried to lift Braden's trunk to move it, Brenna lay a hand on the man's arm.

"The trunk stays."

The Fraser man nodded and departed the chambers without it. Brenna looked at Dawn and her uncle.

"Not yet," she told them.

***

The flurry of the day left them covered in a film of dust and bone-achingly tired. And there was still more to do for Brenna's refurnished chambers on the morrow.

A fine supper of tender venison and boiled leeks called Brenna downstairs, and though a number of her mother's kirtles and gowns now hung on pegs in her fresh chambers, 'twas enough change for Brenna. She opened the trunk and put on one of her brother's tunics for supper.

Instead of sitting with her uncle, she found a seat at the table next to Rafe, who lifted a fat chalice at her. His easy, handsome smile widened as he spoke.

"I hear congratulations are in order."

Brenna squinted at him. "For what?"

"I overheard Kellan mention he'd spent the day moving items from your mother's chambers into yours. A new table and gowns? Are ye getting ready to fly?"

His eyes held a tease, and a heated blush rose from Brenna's chest to her cheeks. The hall suddenly seemed overly hot. Her brother's woolen tunic and bonnet were heavy and oppressive. Rafe leaned into her, noting her embarrassment.

"'Tis naught to be ashamed of. It may take a while, but 'twill happen. Just wait."

He sipped his celebratory wine. Brenna tilted her head at him.

"How did ye ken? That I was no' ready? How do ye ken that it takes time? Did ye wait for something? To leave for the Bruce, perchance?"

Rafe choked on his wine, spitting it out in a burgundy mess that dripped down his chin. He coughed and his eyes watered. Brenna pounded on his back while the other Frasers at the table watched with mild interest.

Once he caught his breath and wiped his sleeve across his face, he waved Brenna's arm away.

"I'm fine," he choked in explanation. "I swallowed wrong."

Brenna's features went flat, waiting for her answer.

"I'm sorry. Ye were saying?" Rafe asked.

"How do ye ken it takes time? Did ye wait until ye were ready to join the Bruce? Is that why ye are no' with your men?"

Oh, the lies he'd told, this thick forest of lies that grew only more dense with each telling. If she ever discovered the truth, she'd never forgive him. He'd told far too many untruths — it made her lie about her identity seem like a fairy story.

Especially since, as of late, he'd found himself thinking more and more of this skittish lass, the naked image of her emerging from the loch, their heartfelt conversations . . .

He shook his head.

"Aye," he answered in a furtive tone, his eyes averted. "I had to wait."

Rafe finished his wine and left the hall.

Chapter Nine: New Chambers

RAFE DIDN'T RETURN to the keep that night — who would miss him? Instead, he found a soft pile of hay in the barn and curled up with the animals. It served him right. He was as base as the goats and chickens for living a lie with these kind people who'd taken him in.

When were the Bruce Frasers supposed to come back to Broch Invershin? Brenna had told him they were to come home soon. Was that a fortnight? A month? Rafe's burning mind was nearly spent — he wasn't certain how much longer he'd be able to live this sham.

Duncan and his cronies had their doubts since the day they'd met Rafe. And they shared those doubts with the Laird and his brother, that was clear enough. He'd seen how Robert studied him under a hooded gaze when they were in the same room. Rafe was shocked they didn't have a Fraser follow him to the barn.

The worst part was what he was doing to poor Brenna. She was coming to terms with the death of her brother and mother, emerging from her shell with the help of Rafe, of all people, and every word that fell from his lips was soaked with falsehood. Whenever he looked that fair woman in the face, he was deceiving her.

Yet she didn't know, and when her innocent eyes gazed up at him, rested on him with a sense of security, it struck as a twisting knife in his heart. 'Twas strange, that he'd believed her to be a lad when they first met, even in her poor costume. However, once she was revealed as a woman, he hadn't been able to control his thoughts around her. Her father should be grateful she hid as a lad for as long as she had — otherwise the clan might have a larger problem of unbidden suitors competing for the hand of the beautiful, only daughter of the Frasers of Loch Laro. How had no one seen those refined lines, those captivating eyes, those gracious curves, that glorious hair under a bonnet?

He continued to allow the memory of her dripping, nubile body to infiltrate his mind, the touch of her lips from their kiss to kindle a fire in his loins. Other than the blonde kitchen maid, Brenna was the closest thing to a friend he had here, or to any friend he could trust in a long while. He well understood why she hid — he did the same. Perchance 'twas that they were so much alike that compelled his heart.

The time they'd spent together since her misadventure in the woods consumed him. He needed to stay away — he was lying about his identity and was in no position to fall in love with anyone, least of all the Laird's daughter. He tried to tell himself the quivering that overwhelmed him when she was near was not a result of his desire for her. That the excitement pulsing in his veins when she sought him out, even just to greet him, was not because he had any emotional connection. But he was doing what he did best.

Lying.

He was lying to himself if he said he had no feelings for her.

Rafe had fallen for the Laird's daughter, and all her brokenness and quirks, in a way he hadn't thought possible. Fallen hard. Fallen in love.

He loved every part of her — her strange dress, her short sun-burnt hair, her wide smile, and her amber eyes that flared like a fire when she looked upon him. A glance could bring Rafe, the powerful MacKay warrior, to his knees.

And the more his thoughts strayed to Brenna and the way she watched him, the more he wanted her. What was he to do? Leave? Admit the truth? Chase his heart? He tossed and turned in his covers.

The gentle rustling of barn animals lulled him to sleep, and when he dreamed, he dreamed of Brenna.

***

The bustling of the village coming to life woke Rafe, and he stumbled from the barn to the yard. He'd taken to sleeping in the barn after too many close moments with Brenna. The pull she had on him was too great, and when he was in the keep, so close yet so far, he feared his lack of control. The barn was cooler, safer, with fewer Frasers, and no Brenna.

After finding vittles to break his fast and working with Kellan to tend the very animals he had bedded with the night before, Rafe came to the conclusion 'twould be better if he departed in search of the Bruce's army on his own. If he left for the Lowlands today, Rafe could find the Bruce's army in a few days' time. Though he grappled with the decision, he was assured of this plan. In the end, the risk of remaining with the Frasers, of falling even harder for the Laird's odd daughter, of being discovered, was too terrible to contemplate.

He was waiting until his work for the day was finished before gathering his meager belongings, and with luck, several oatcakes and dried fish from Dawn in the kitchen. He could leave on the morn.

The only problem was man plans and God laughs.

He was laying his pitchfork aside when Brenna, dressed as Bren, found him in the barn.

"Rafe! I've been searching for ye. I have something I want to show ye."

She held out a dainty hand, and Rafe stared at it.

His brain screamed at him to ignore it, to turn away from that milky invitation and leave.

Everything else inside him screamed louder. His heart pounded in his chest, bruising it from the inside. He sighed heavily with defeat, and almost against his will, took her hand. Nay, not against his will, for he had none when it came to Brenna. He couldn't explain it, but with Brenna, he was lost. A subtle grin tugged at his cheeks.

"What do ye want to show me?"

"Your words, I took them to heart." Her face brightened as she spoke. "Ye are right. I've had six years to grieve. If I continue, I will end up no better off than my poor father. I need to start finding out how to live as myself and no' hide from the world. So, with Dawn and my uncle's help over the past week, we did something. I've started to emerge from my cocoon."

He furrowed his brow at her request and followed her up the steps, deep into the keep, to the door of an upstairs chamber.

"What's this?"

"My chambers. Come."

Rafe yanked his hand away as she opened the door. She turned back to him with an expression of confusion under her slouchy bonnet. *What fresh temptation was this?*

"'Tis inappropriate," he explained in a tight voice. Why did she want him in her room?

"Nay, 'tis something ye need to see. Ye helped do this. Your words gave me the first step I needed to finish my grieving. Look."

The door swung open. He peeked his head in while keeping his feet on the hall side of the threshold.

'Twas a woman's chambers. A neat bed topped with fresh furs and plaids. A pair of colorful gowns hung from pegs at the foot of the bed. A dainty ingrained wood table sat against the wall and was home to a set of combs and water bowl. The only things out of place were a worn trunk near the hearth and a set of dirks that lay under a surprisingly refined portrait of a woman. A woman who bore a striking resemblance to Brenna.

She noticed how he stared at it and stepped next to Rafe. Grabbing his arm, she tugged him closer, encouraging him to enter the room, and without thinking or any sense of willpower, he obeyed.

"My mother," she said, her breathy voice warm against his cheek, and only then did he realize how close they stood. "She died of heartbreak shortly after my brother passed. I would no' have known this painting existed but for your words."

Rafe raised a slow eyebrow in question, and Brenna told him how she took his advice to heart, and entered her mother's room for the first time in six years, and how her uncle Robert had put the painting in her mother's chambers where Brenna found it. How she removed it and several of her mother's items to her brother's chambers, now her chambers, and began creating her own sanctuary out of her brother's room.

Brenna removed her bonnet from her bronze fluff of hair and tossed it on her bed. Then she faced Rafe, taking both of his coarse hands in her own. Her wide, shining eyes searched his, and Rafe fell into them, lost again.

"I would no' have this image of my mother. I would no' have worked to make my brother's chambers more of a place for me. Yet when ye talked of butterflies, it spoke to me in a way I hadn't been able to hear in a long time. I dinna know why, but when ye speak to me, it reaches me in a manner I've no' experienced before."

She swiveled her head around the room, an expression of tempered joy putting roses on her cheeks.

"Ye helped me do this. And I thank ye."

Before he realized what was happening, her arms were around his neck and her gentle, innocent lips were on his.

He should have pushed her away. His mind screamed at him to unwrap her arms and leave the room. And he meant to — in his head, he told himself he would.

But God help him, instead he enclosed her waist in his hands and kissed her back. He lost himself even more.

As their lips and tongue parried and danced, a familiar and urgent heat built in Rafe. He clutched Brenna to his chest and let one hand slip lower, where her loose braies gathered at her backside, and cupped one tight curve of her buttocks.

She moaned into his mouth but didn't pull away. Instead, she clung to him, her hands squeezing at his hard muscles under his tunic.

A fire ignited in his loins which pressed against her soft body, begging for succor. He reached his other hand down to her buttocks and lifted her into his hips. Brenna squealed at the movement, and realization of where he was and who he was with struck him like a hammer. Rafe thrust her away and stumbled toward the door. What was he doing?

"Rafe. What —? Did I do something wrong?"

He tried to gain control of his erratic breathing. He kept his head lowered, his eyes hooded.

"Nay, lass. That's the problem. Ye did everything right. But ye are just finding yourself, coming out of your grief, and I am no' a man to take advantage of a lass in a compromised state. And I —"

Rafe stopped himself. The longing in his body begged him to stay, to keep her wrapped in his arms. He wished to tell her who he truly was, be honest the same way she had opened up to him, yet he couldn't. Not with how she looked at him with those dulcet amber eyes. She was too fragile for that yet.

"I should leave," he said instead, trying to soften his response to her. "Your chambers, they are lovely. Your brother and mother would be proud. Ye should show your father. It might bring him joy as well."

Brenna didn't speak but nodded at his advice. The look of confusion on her face was enough to wrench his heart.

Rafe stepped into the hall and rushed for the yard. He needed fresh air to clear his head and calm his raging need.

This was everything Rafe didn't want. He'd left the MacKays because they were a lying, conniving clan, and here he was, lying and conniving.

He'd left to find his own way with the Bruce, and instead he tumbled onto a fragile young woman who had no idea of the effect she had on him. In braies or skirts, 'twouldn't matter. Something in that lass called to him, and by God, he wanted to answer.

***

Brenna stood stock-still as she watched Rafe leave the room in a swish of plaid. Run from the room was more like it.

And in truth, confusion consumed Brenna. Ever since Rafe arrived, her emotions had roiled inside her, a tempest in her mind and chest. For years she'd been content to assume the role of a lad, live her brother's life cut short. 'Twas accepted by her clan, even protected by the warriors her uncle had assigned her.

Why did the arrival of this dark stranger shift her world? Why was it suddenly important to leave her youthful peculiarities behind and retake her role as the Laird's daughter?

And more importantly, what was she supposed to do now?

Should she pursue the MacLeod man? He'd responded to her kiss with fervor, at first. To what end? Would her uncle even let her wed some unknown stranger?

Wed? Why was that now a thought in her head?

And did she want to marry at all? Or could she just be with him, perchance satiate her curiosity and quell the wantonness that he wrought inside her? Then resume her life of respectability?

Brenna was frozen in her thoughts, trying to figure out why she couldn't control her feelings, couldn't make a decision. She needed to find the right step to take next.

But in who could she confide? Not her uncle. 'Twas not the type of exchange she could have with the man who had stepped in to be a father to her. And not Anne — 'twould be the same as telling Robert.

Not her own father. He would no sooner have an answer than he could recall her name on the first try. Or the second.

Her tense eyes skipped around the room as she struggled with her thoughts, and her eyes landed on the portrait of her mother. It hadn't happened often, but as she had grown into adulthood, she'd experienced more moments where her mother would be the person she wanted to go to.

Her heart lurched at that thought, and on the cusp of her sadness, an idea struck her.

Dawn had been so kind to help her start this journey to shed her brother's skin and find her own. She was a woman Brenna might trust, a woman who might have advice for a young lass who had no idea how to be a lass.

Her eyes flicked to the gowns that hung on the pegs, and then at the clothes she was wearing. For a conversation like this, she needed comfort. She wasn't ready to wear a gown. Not yet.

***

Dawn worked in the kitchens with Sarah and Dorcas, her sleeves shoved up above her elbows as she kneaded a thick round of oat bread dough. A fine dusting of oat flour coated her arms and sprinkled across her face as pale freckles. She smiled when Brenna walked up to the wooden workspace.

"Are ye taking a break from following Nevan and Kellan around to join me? Would ye like to make some oatcakes?"

Dawn didn't wait for a response and threw a lump of dough her way. Then she tipped her head at Sarah.

"Go wash yourself and join me here."

Dawn had a way of making Brenna feel welcome no matter the task at hand. Sarah handed Brenna a water bowl and cloth, and after she scrubbed the remnants of her moving day from her fingers, she joined Dawn at the dusty table.

Dawn sprinkled a layer of flour over her hands and on the table, then went back to her lump of dough, using her knuckles to bear down into the pliable fluff. Brenna studied her movements and then copied her, digging into her own dough with force.

"Kneading dough is a great way to work out whatever has ye upset. Ye can punch at it, pull at it, work it over and over." Dawn replicated the actions as she spoke them. "Many a time I've wanted to strike someone, so I come in here and attack the dough instead."

The kitchen lasses giggled at Dawn's sentiment. Brenna wondered if her conundrum was evident on her face. For Dawn to suggest she pound on bread dough, it must be. And Dorcas had already spoken with Brenna about her interest in the MacLeod man. Brenna was certain they all had an idea of what was on her mind.

"Can I ask ye a question, Dawn?" Brenna's tentative voice was low and shaky,

Dawn's deft fingers continued their soothing movements, sweeping at the round dough ball to smooth it. "Aye. What ails ye?" Her voice was as soothing as her hands, calm and encouraging.

"Ye made a comment yesterday. Of why I wished to, uh, change my chambers?"

Brenna clenched her jaw and kept her gaze on her dough. This conversation was going to be difficult. Brenna couldn't even bring herself to mention Rafe, or Dawn's suggestive comment about him from earlier.

"Och, that perchance ye want to shed the braies and wear a gown for the new man in our midst?"

Dawn's boldness made Brenna's cheeks burn with embarrassment. She tried to keep her focus on her oatcake dough while the other kitchen maids stopped their giggling and wormed their way closer to eavesdrop.

"Um, aye. I'm no longer a secret, so he kens who I am. He kens of the death of my mother and brother, and a bit about my father's illness. He's been kind and understanding over, well . . ." She gestured at her tunic.

Dawn flapped a dusty hand at her. "Your manner of dress?" she asked with a smile.

"Aye," Brenna gushed. "For some reason, when he speaks to me, everything just makes sense. And I feel —?" she paused, too ashamed to speak as boldly as Dawn, especially since Sarah and Dorcas were practically falling off their stools to listen.

"We've seen how your eyes shine when ye are near the man, Brenna. 'Tis no secret there."

Brenna snapped her head up, the horror in her mind beaming from her wide eyes. Was she that obvious?

Dawn chuckled at her discomfort.

"Brenna," she leaned over the table to pat Brenna's floured hand with her own. "Things have changed over the past six years. Did ye think ye'd pass as a lad for your whole life?"

Brenna sucked on her lower lip. No, she hadn't, but in truth, she hadn't thought on her future that way. 'Twas enough of a struggle to get through each day. Then once she'd was used to standing in for her brother, she really didn't think on it further. Not until Rafe showed up.

"Has your father spoken to ye about your future or marriage? Or your uncle?"

Smack. Splat. Smack. Splat. Dawn's hands on the dough was a lulling cadence. So casual for such an important conversation. At least to Brenna. She shook her head.

"Nay. Everything's been, weel, ignored, I think. Pushed to the side? And who wants to be with a lass who dresses as a man? Nay. Nothing's been mentioned to me."

Dawn shared a sidelong glance with Sarah and Dorcas, who both giggled again.

"What?" Brenna asked.

Dawn rubbed her floured hand against her chin, coating her in even more white dust.

"True, ye may have dressed as a man, and passed as a lad to drunkards or from a distance. But your clan, we here know ye aren't a lad, aye?"

Brenna studied Dawn, struggling to comprehend her meaning.

"To be honest, ye didn't look that much like a lad as ye grew older. We here, we knew ye a lass all the while. So, even if ye thought ye were hiding, ye weren't. No' so much." Dawn rolled the dough into a round lump in the center of the table. "Touched in the head, mayhap. Ye managed to keep your fine traits that ye had a child, so ye are well liked. At most, the clan, our neighbors believed it to be part of your mourning. A long, long mourning. There are plenty of lads who want to wed ye, daughter of Laird Kevin Fraser of Broch Invershin, braies or nay."

"Ye are a pretty lass," Dorcas piped up from the hearth. Brenna raised her chin at Dorcas, a tight smile on her face.

"But ye did no' know any of this," Dawn continued, "trying to hide from the past as ye were. Finding a man who makes your insides swirl in a fog is no' a bad thing. Sometimes, for a lass, it just takes the right man." More giggling from the hearth. Brenna's blush deepened, her entire face the hue of a Scots wildflower.

"He's a stranger. Does that make a difference?"

Dawn's gaze left the dough that she had rolled flat, and taking Brenna's hand, she stared into her wide eyes.

"'Tis a bit of a problem. Your uncle, your guards, Duncan and his ilk, they will no' accept the man until they know everything about him. They will no' want him wooing ye until they are certain who he is, know more of his clan and family. He may be dangerous, or only want ye because of your position as the daughter of the

Laird. These things, they will want to discover every secret the man might have."

Dawn dropped Brenna's hand and grabbed a cup, using the lip to cut circles in the dough.

"From how ye blush every time Rafe's name is mentioned, I think 'tis too late to keep the man from ye."

This time, Brenna's face burned red. How did Dawn read her so well? And to suggest such a thing out loud? Dawn giggled like Sarah and Dorcas, and gave Brenna's hand another motherly pat.

"If he's the man who has opened your heart, I for one dinna think he can be dangerous. Your uncle may see the value of that as well. Ye are coming out of your shell for the first time in years, and those who care for ye are pleased to see it. Especially your uncle. They might be grateful to Rafe. If ye want this man, who are we to tell ye nay?"

Brenna poked at the lump of dough in front of her. 'Twasn't the advice she thought she'd receive, but Dawn's words were sage, and from the happy nods of the lassies across the kitchen, Dawn had the right of it.

Brenna did want Rafe — she wanted to know more about him, feel the warmth and security of his arms around her, lose herself in the manliness of him. Mayhap she'd needed someone like him, an outsider who could stand as a gatekeeper between her and this frightening world that had treated her so harshly. Who could hold her hand as she tried to walk this journey of life out in the open once more.

Her heart spoke louder than any doubts or fears she had.

Rafe was that man.

Chapter Ten: Duncan's Revelations

"ROBERT, I MUST SPEAK with ye about the visitor Brenna brought home," Duncan told Robert as he walked into the Laird's study.

The Laird-in-standing rolled his eyes heavenward. On top of Brenna's near miss, hearing more strife regarding the MacLeod man only added to Robert's list of concerns.

"I can only imagine the depth of misery your assignment to my niece has been. I appreciate your continued guard over her as she prances around in a lad's clothing. It can no' have been easy. And now, with this dark man she brought home like a lost puppy. How did she manage to pull that one over on ye, again?"

Robert sat behind a desk of polished ash, several papers, a pot of ink, and a quill littering the top. The papers and documents were the worst part of standing in for his brother, who as of late had only grown worse. Robert was at his wit's end of how to care for a man who no longer knew anyone who entered his room, and his heart ached for his loss and for Brenna's. No wonder she behaved so erratically. If Robert had lost everything when he was but a bairn, who's to say he wouldn't have behaved the same?

Duncan grunted at the question and sat wearily into the wooden chair opposite Robert.

"He's been naught but a prince since he's been here," Duncan admitted. "A solid man to count on. A friend to Brenna, and even saved her life and rumors say he helped start that room change, so he seems trustworthy. Yet, something is off. I canna place my finger on it, but something."

Robert set his papers to the side and leaned forward on this desktop, his face full of sharp focus. Duncan was a thoughtful man. Whenever Duncan spoke, Robert listened.

"Like what?"

"He's too close to Brenna. That troubles me. But worse, the man does no' answer to his own name."

Robert's brow knitted, and he sat up tall in his chair. This problem was not unfamiliar to him or Duncan. When Brenna had announced that she no longer wanted to be called Brenna, but Bren, a boy's name like her brother's, they had laughed politely and indulged her. But it took a long time, months in fact, before she began to respond to it as her name.

If Rafe MacLeod was no' answering to his name, what name did he answer to?

"I did no' notice this," Robert began, and Duncan held up a hand.

"He answers to Rafe. The man was clever enough to keep his first name, I believe. He does no' answer to MacLeod. When I ask him about it, he claims to be 'woolgathering.'"

Blood pounded in a fury inside Robert's skull. They had welcomed a stranger into their clan, into their family, into wee Brenna's life, and he was lying about who he was. Both men were now on edge.

"Keep your eye on him. We need to find out who he is."

Duncan inclined his head. "I have either myself or Kellan on the man at all times. But I have a possible way to learn more, if he is who he says he is."

Robert leaned back and folded his hands on his broad chest. "I'm listening."

"I have a MacLeod cousin. Distant kin, but kin nonetheless, on my mother's side. I have no' visited in a time. I'll head out later today and ask if he kens any Rafe MacLeod."

"But Rafe may no' be from that clan. The MacLeods litter the western seaboard."

"True, but if Gavin kens the man, it at least gives us something. If he doesn't, then we must investigate more."

Robert nodded his assent. "'Tis a sound idea. Task Kellan to keep his eye on this Rafe whilst ye are gone."

Duncan rose to leave, and Robert stood with him.

"And Duncan?"

Duncan half-turned to Robert.

"Thank ye again for your fierce commitment to the Laird and his daughter. Ye are truly a loyal man."

Duncan gave a bow and left.

Robert collapsed into his seat, his entire body hot with irritation. He pressed the palms of his hands against his eyes, trying to control himself. Then he stood again and raced from the study.

***

Duncan's journey west took just under a day, his steed noble and stalwart the entire ride and his claymore strapped to his back, at the ready. Should he encounter any bandits or those devils the MacKays, Duncan would have a gift for them they'd not forget.

However, the grass and stone-littered road, which was really more of a trail through the brush, was quiet. Only the sounds of birds and scuttling animals reached his ears. He was the only man riding that day, it seemed to Duncan.

The MacLeod lands rose before him, the stronghold a welcome sight in the sunset after a day's ride. If he were lucky, Duncan had arrived in time to eat as he conversed with his cousin. If he were even more fortunate, he might find a willing lass to keep him warm under his plaids. While strange, his duties as guard for Bren were easy, but they didn't permit for much time with the lassies unless he snuck away after Bren found his chambers early in the night.

That didn't happen often enough for a randy man like Duncan. He thanked the stars that he had Kellan and Nevan to fill in guard duty, otherwise Duncan might find himself becoming a monk. Celibacy did not suit Highland warriors, Duncan decided.

A pair of kerchiefed women were digging in the dirt with their spades, hacking at parsnips clinging tight to the earth. They barely raised their faces as he approached.

"Good day, ye fine women!" Duncan called out as his horse halted near them. "I am Duncan Fraser, from Broch Invershin. My kin, Gavin, is he within the keep?"

One woman gave him a disinterested shrug, while the other woman pointed to the side of the manse.

"'Tis close to the evening meal. If he's nay in the hall, ye may find him in the stables."

Duncan bowed his head in thanks and continued toward the keep. From the cacophony echoing within the hall, Duncan assumed he'd find both food and his cousin there.

Hobbling his horse near the steps, he made his way to the large, double door entry. A goodish number of men and women clad in all manner of woolen gowns, tunics, and plaids gathered at the tables, their cheery voices a pleasing respite from the oft dire reminders of his own clan's ill luck. He stepped in unnoticed, scanning for a solid man with sandy brown hair.

Gavin MacLeod sat at a low table close to the front of the hall, a fair blonde woman serving him from a pitcher. They shared a deep kiss, causing the rest of those at the table to call out bawdy cheers at their romantic antics. A wry smile pulled at Duncan's lips.

So his cousin found a woman to put up with his more stoic personality. Good man.

Gavin didn't notice Duncan until he stood at the foot of the table, then leapt at the giant man. They shared a quick embrace before Gavin stood back, looking up at his cousin.

Their Nordic features and shared, aquiline noses bespoke of a rich Viking heritage, and they appeared as blonde mountains among men.

"Duncan! 'Tis a joy to see ye, man!" Gavin pounded Duncan on his back and handed him a tankard of bubbly mead. "Come join us for our evening meal!"

Duncan sat next to Gavin, squeezing his girth onto the edge of the bench. "I thought ye'd never ask, ye lout!"

He dug in, not having eaten a bite since that morning when he'd departed. The rich scent of venison stew made his mouth water. The same blonde who'd kissed Gavin returned with a bowl of stew and set it before Duncan with a wooden spoon. Then she was gone before he could say a word. Duncan flicked his spoon in the direction the lassie had gone and raised a bushy eyebrow in his cousin's direction. Gavin laughed, his face set with pride.

"Pretty lass, eh? I hope to wed her in the fall. She's my Jenny."

Duncan dug into his bowl. "I did no' think ye had it in ye."

Gavin shoved Duncan lightly with his shoulder before slurping up his own stew.

"What brings ye to MacLeod land? More than a social visit, I expect?" Gavin asked around a mouthful of venison.

"How did ye ken?"

Gavin cut his eye sidelong to his cousin. "Your face is tighter, nay as rakish as usual. And ye did no' ask about an available lass when ye first sat down. If ye are no' asking about women, something must be amiss."

Duncan chewed slowly, considering his words. Gavin didn't know everyone in his clan, and what if Rafe was from a different clan of MacLeods? The man had been vague with details of his home and family, and Duncan's trip to see Gavin may have been naught more than a goose chase.

"We accidentally brought home a stranger," Duncan began. Gavin said nothing, continuing to eat. Having guests in one's home was a Highland tradition. "He says he's a MacLeod."

Gavin's face leveled at Duncan, trying to figure out his cousin's concern. "And?"

Duncan wiped his face with the corner of his plaid. "And I dinna think he's a MacLeod."

Gavin stiffened, his spoon held in mid-air, and his features grew rigid.

"Ye think he's hiding his identity?"

"Aye, and I must be sure, as much as I can be. Do ye ken a Rafe MacLeod in the MacLeods of Lochnora or with distant kin?"

"How important is this?" Gavin set his spoon aside.

"He's become verra close with the only child of our Laird rather quickly. We've had much misery these past years. We can no' have a man take advantage of the Laird or our clan."

Gavin nodded knowingly. 'Twasn't a clan in the Highlands who didn't know of the Frasers of Broch Invershin. And who didn't send up private prayers of thanks that such misery didn't afflict them?

"Wait here," Gavin directed.

He rose in a blur of blue-green plaid and rushed the next table over, where a confident, black-haired man sat next to a dainty, sunset-hued woman. Laird Ewan MacLeod and his wife, Meg. A bairn of less than a year sat on Meg's lap, slapping at a plate of pottage. Duncan had missed seeing them when he first entered the hall.

Gavin's light head dipped low to Ewan's raven locks, speaking into the man's ear. Ewan's bright eyes glanced over at Duncan, who gave the Laird a quick bow of his head in recognition. Then the Laird's attention focused on Gavin's words.

They spoke briefly, then Gavin returned to his spot on the bench.

"My Laird does no' recall a Rafe MacLeod, and nay do I. But that does no' mean the man is no' who he claims to be. A fair number of MacLeods litter the west and the isles. He may well be a man we dinna ken."

"But ye dinna ken any Rafe MacLeod."

Gavin shook his head. "Nay, cousin. I dinna ken any man by that name."

Duncan wasn't sure if he was relieved or more concerned. He achieved his goal, to ask Gavin about their black-haired stranger, and now he could enjoy the remainder of his visit with his kin.

"I appreciate your time, cousin," Duncan told him, then resumed slurping his stew.

After the evening meal, the night wore down and Gavin made to leave with his woman, Jenny. Before departing the hall, he bid Duncan good eve and gave him a sound recommendation.

"The black-haired lass yonder? She is a woman whom ye may find friendly enough this eve."

Gavin winked at Duncan, then escorted his bride-to-be from the hall to find their own diversions.

Duncan grinned to himself as the pair left. He could always count on Gavin to find a willing lass.

Any lingering thoughts of the MacLeod stranger disappeared as the dark-haired beauty eagerly agreed to follow Duncan to a shadowy corner of the hall.

And as he slipped his cockstand between her yielding thighs, all other concerns flew from his head as well, until there was nothing else in the world except the woman's warm sheath and his own rising passion.

Once he lost himself, he collapsed in a breathless hulk. Shifting beside the woman (her name was Marie, so noble sounding), he curled around her back and kept one arm over her midsection. His hand rested on the soft curve of her breast, and he fell asleep thinking he must have died and gone to heaven.

It'd been far too long since he'd fallen asleep with a lass in his arms.

Duncan rode off just after sunrise with a belly full of eggs and parritch and his lips tasting of a jet-haired lass.

'Twas enough of a diversion. Now 'twas time to relay what he'd learned to Robert.

Chapter Eleven: Less than Noble Intentions

RAFE SHOULD HAVE been surprised when she came to him that night, dressed in naught but her shift.

When Brenna's kinsmen called her bullheaded, they weren't wrong. Whether 'twas in her desire to wear men's clothing, to hide from the world, or to get the man she wanted, Brenna was nothing but staunch in her will. As misguided as it might be.

If he'd thought her frail, he was mistaken. Brenna did what she wanted, regardless of what others said. He only had to look at her dress and behaviors when he first met the Frasers. And how anyone thought her a young lad, no matter what she wore, was a mystery to him. He'd known from the first that something was amiss. Had he looked deeper, 'twould have been obvious. She could not have hidden that luscious body for long.

He groaned and rolled over on his back, the stuffed hay pallet crinkling under his backside.

The barn door squeaked as someone entered. Rafe tucked himself into the shadows of a stall, hiding until a light voice spoke into the darkness.

"Rafe? Are ye within?"

Brenna. What was she doing here? Didn't she know how inappropriate 'twas for the two of them to be alone? Especially after that kiss.

At first he had a mind to keep quiet. She tip-toed farther into the barn, and a goose squawked at her presence. She'd bring the entire Fraser clan upon them if he didn't stop her.

"Lass, I am here. What brings ye to the barn this time of night?"

There was only one reason he knew for a woman to search out a man late at night, but he couldn't imagine that Brenna was here for that.

Even if her fingers had lingered on his arm.

Even if her lips had searched his with an ardent fervor that brought him to the brink.

Even if her body clung to him, and she hadn't pushed his hands away when they gripped her backside.

Then she stepped into a shaft of moonlight, wrapped in a plaid cape against the chill in the air. When she dropped the plaid to her feet, she stood in nothing but her creamy shift. She was as pale as a spirit, a spirit of passion and yearning that commanded his cock to throb unwillingly.

"Ye do. Ye bring me here," she whispered into the darkness.

Rafe's brain screamed at him to deny this woman, to tell her to return to her newly refreshed chambers and search for herself there, not find herself under his thrusting hips. He demanded that his mouth command her to depart, leave him to his own sad, dishonest self, confess that he was not the man she thought he was or wanted him to be.

Instead, his baser nature won out. His hands reached for her curvy body under that thin film of fabric and guided her lips to his mouth, where he captured her mouth in a devouring kiss that belied his true desires.

Hidden and grieving though she may have been, this woman and her clan were everything the MacKays were not, and he could thrive here. Maybe return to Loch Laro after his time with the Bruce, but they might never accept him if they learned he was not who he claimed and had his way with the Laird's daughter.

This dervish of thoughts burned in his mind as his hands slipped beneath her shift, skipping his fingertips over her smooth skin. Brenna inhaled deeply and pulled herself upright.

Her eyes glowed as torches in the night, roving over his slick raven curls and eyes as blue as a summer sky. She raised a finger to his face, tracing the contours of his cheek and jaw, then dropping to his bare chest, where his hard muscles clenched under her touch. Her fingertip drew lines over one side of his chest to the other, twirling through the light thatch of downy black hair that spread across his chest and down the sharp definition of his stomach, like an arrow pointing its way home.

He didn't breathe while her fingers discovered the expanse of his body, afraid that if he did, he would break the moment and scare this bronze goddess away.

As her hands moved to his stomach, his own hands caressed her ribs to the curve of her breasts, still covered from his sight. He panted, his desire to see those wanton globes, see the glory of her naked body churning an ache deep inside him.

His thumbs reached her pert nipples, ripe and inviting, and her hand froze on his stomach. Her eyes widened with surprise, and it was that subtle shift of her gaze that brought him to his senses. He pulled his hand from under her gown and clasped her fingers to his chest.

"Lass," he choked out, hating the words that he must say. "I canna have ye here. 'Tis no' safe for ye here."

"What do I have to be afeared of?" she asked breathlessly.

Oh, this innocent had no idea of the beast that raged under his skin, an animal that wanted to lash out with a roar and take her right here in the barn. Rafe suppressed the growl that rumbled in his chest.

"Me, lass. Ye are just coming out of a long period of grieving. Ye are trying to find yourself again. 'Twould be too easy for a man such as me to take ye in a moment of weakness. And I want to, dinna get me wrong. I want to take advantage of ye as I've never wanted another woman before. And that is what ye need to be afeared of. 'Tis why ye must leave."

Brenna's sat in silence on his lap as their eyes held each other's gaze, blue against bronze. He didn't remove his hands, holding one breast against his palm and her hand against his chest with the other. When she tried to pull her arm back, his grip tightened, clasping her. She inhaled sharply at her captive state.

Rafe growled again, then released her and rested his hands in the hay at his sides.

"That is why ye must leave," he whispered in a hoarse voice. She yanked her hand away like it was on fire.

He believed if he could scare her away, then she would leave in an offended huff and not return. But as she started to rise, she leaned forward to catch his lips in a sudden kiss. In a flash his hand was at the back of her head, crushing their mouths together. Then she pushed him backwards, and he tumbled into the hay.

"Ye may no' think me ready. Or this no' the right time. 'Tis only *not yet*," she commanded with authority as she stood over him, a queen reigning over her subject.

Then she snatched her plaid from where it had fallen in the hay and departed — a wisp of color in the dark.

Rafe let his head fall back with the rest of him and covered his eyes with his arm. He took several deep breaths, trying to calm the storm Brenna had wrought in his mind and in his loins.

How did she affect him so? Why did this lass who, until recently had pretended to be someone else, embrace who she was becoming with such vigor and haste that she had the audacity to come to him at night?

He was playing with fire. So was she. He vowed to leave first thing in the morn.

***

But Kellan grabbed Rafe from the hay before he fully awoke and shoved a quick breakfast of kippers and oatcakes at him as they rode out to where the Fraser Clan kept their fluffy Highland cattle. Three other Fraser men rode with them — Rafe nodded at their introductions as they trotted past the trees to an open field in the glen. The cattle pasture.

"When the cattle lads retrieved the herd last night, 'twere four milking heifers missing. The lads counted twice, and after they brought the cattle back to their pens, they returned and found horse tracks. They reported this back to Nevan, who took the information to Robert. He ordered me to take some men and investigate."

So much for leaving on the morn. Why does he want me to join them? Rafe pondered as he fastened his kilt and wrapped his plaid around his shoulders while they rode.

"I would have thought Duncan was going to join us," Rafe said, noting he hadn't seen the giant circling Brenna for the past day. Since the man had made it a mission to keep an eye on Brenna, and thus on Rafe, his absence seemed odd.

"He's visiting family west o' here. He has a close cousin who was raised with him, and he visits often," Kellan responded,

148

keeping his eyes straight ahead, searching for the tracks the cattle lads had mentioned.

"There," one of the other riders called out, pointing north of the field.

They dismounted to investigate on feet and followed the tracks, which included horse hoof prints and cattle tracks, to where they disappeared into the trampled grasses north. Kellan squatted low to the muddy dirt, studying the tracks.

"Four or five riders, and look," he pointed toward the tree-lined moorlands that stretched north. A heavy, sinking sensation clutched Rafe's chest in an icy grip. He knew where those tracks led. So did Kellan. "They lead to MacKay lands. They sure took their time coming back."

Rafe remained quiet and hung back behind a shorter Fraser man. A single wrong word could lead to his discovery, and now that his clan was again wreaking havoc on the Frasers, he needed to keep his identity hidden all the more. He cursed under his breath. He should have left for the Bruce yesterday. Why did he keep getting caught up with the Frasers and delaying his departure? But then, he knew the answer to that question.

"Shall we follow the tracks? Or report back?" the short Fraser asked. Kellan's eyes narrowed and studied the landscape. His face was hard with wrath.

"I dinna ken where the MacKays may be and dinna want to lead us into an ambush. Let's head back."

The Frasers and Rafe moved with quick stealth to their horses and rode to Broch Invershin.

Rafe acted with haste and was crouched in the walled off area at the rear of the main hall, packing his belongings, when Brenna found him.

"Rafe?" she asked in a tentative voice, and he set his sporran down before turning to face her.

He froze mid-turn.

The Bren character was gone. Completely gone. In his place stood Brenna — not in rough, baggy braies and a tunic that nigh reached her knees, but in a soft bark-brown woolen gown with a scooped neck and a low waist. A chain dangled at her full hips and a red and black *arasaid* was thrown over her shoulders and draped down her back. Her shorter hair, uncommon for a Highland lass, was loose, nary a bonnet to hide her shiny bronzed tresses that fell in wispy locks against her shoulders.

She was the embodiment of feminine beauty, a butterfly emerging in its glory from its cocoon. And she stole his breath from his chest and the air from the room. Rafe wasn't sure he would ever start breathing again.

"Lass," he said in a breathless whisper, "I almost did no' recognize ye."

A rosy blush tinged her cheeks and ran from her hair to the scooped neck of her gown. Her wide eyes dropped to her skirts, then caught Rafe's gaze.

"Are ye busy now?" She flicked her eyes to his sleeping pallet where his meager belongings lay. "I would have ye join me."

Rafe's lips pursed into a smirk and he crossed his arms over his wide, muscled chest.

"Join ye where?"

Caution was the better part of valor after last night. There was risk in any invitation.

"Will ye join me?" Her dainty features screwed up at him in question, but her will was not to be denied.

His brain screamed *no*. He was on a precipice and his mind, what little reason he had left, demanded he decline the invitation and leave. *No. Just leave.*

Her gaze, though. Those innocent eyes, her soft voice, the shock of her dress, and his own will flew from him. Against his better judgment, Rafe succumbed to his sordid desires and foolish ideals. How frail the flesh was.

He sighed at his own weakness and followed her. Instead of leaving out the front hall, Brenna walked him out through the kitchens. At first Rafe assumed Brenna wanted him there, until she grabbed a sack off the table and kept that swift pace out the rear doorway. She led him northeast.

After only a short distance, Rafe realized they were heading toward the loch where he first learned her secret. *Did she want to go for a swim?* The thought of her naked flesh made his manhood flex with anticipation.

The trees thinned to a narrow clearing, bright sunlight chasing away any shadows. The verdant leaves and thick grass cast the clearing in a green glow, and the entire scene was almost too perfect.

Brenna unwound her tartan from her shoulders and set it on the ground. Then she sat on it, arranging her skirts as she did so.

Rafe could tell she was not used to maneuvering in skirts. Once she settled, she patted the bright red plaid across from her.

Rafe sat obediently, humoring her. From the sack, she withdrew a skin of wine and several chunks of hard cheese.

"What is all this?" Rafe finally asked as he accepted the skin and swallowed. He had the sense he needed as much wine as possible to survive Brenna's machinations.

"Here is where we first met," she told him, tipping her head when he lifted an eyebrow at her. "Weel, where ye met Brenna, nay Bren," she clarified.

"And why did ye bring me here?"

"Ye have learned much of my family, our clan, and while ye've told me bits and pieces, I dinna ken much of ye."

Rafe stilled. He'd managed to avoid most conversations that had focused on himself, giving vague answers or changing the subject. Now here he was, under her scrutiny, at the mercy of her questions. What might she ask? He hardened his face, again that sinking sense of regret filling him for not leaving early in the morning when he had the opportunity.

"What do ye want to know?" he asked, popping a piece of cheese between his lips, trying to appear nonplussed.

"I know of your mother and father. Do ye have sisters or brothers?"

Ahh, an easy question. "Nay. My mother died when I was a bairn. My father did no' handle having a young son well. I was raised more or less in my auntie's family when he started to drink too much. He became little more than a drunkard, but I loved him anyway, drunk or no." He caught Brenna's sympathetic gaze. "I guess we have that in common. Indisposed fathers."

"Aye," she conceded. "Do ye miss him? Did the pain lessen?"

"Aye," Rafe lifted his head to the heavens. "But he was well into his cups. I think he's in a better place now, which helped the pain when it was fresh. 'Tis much less painful to talk of him now. What of your father?"

Rafe took the chance to shift the focus of the conversation.

"My father?" Brenna's lips pulled down as she considered. "Nay. Dawn and his maid, Anne, they are in agreement with my uncle. No' many ken this," Brenna's said as she leaned into him. "But my father's not ill, not like with a cough or the gripe. Something's wrong in his head. He's losing his memories. He lives in the past much of the time, and he canna be trusted by himself. 'Tis only a matter of time before my uncle steps up as Laird in full. I think he's delaying it. Because once he does, it means my father is no' coming back at all."

She spoke so matter-of-factly, it shocked Rafe. What daughter spoke of a beloved parent so casually?

One who had already come to terms with the circumstances, he told himself. No wonder she'd lived in her false identity for so long. Her loss didn't have an end date — it lingered as her father's illness lingered. And the secretive nature of the Laird's "illness" that Dawn had touched on now made sense.

Brenna sighed deeply. Then she tossed her bronze locks, and a slim smile crossed her lips.

"Is that the reason ye decided to join the Bruce? Your father? That loss?"

Ooch, his plan that had gone so awry since meeting this lass. She presented as such a puzzle, and he was drawn into her mystery. Not that 'twas a great plan to begin with, joining the Bruce. Yet, it had been a plan.

"One reason. I was also just tired of doing the same thing every day with my clan. I did no' get along with that. With the Bruce, I've the chance to be a better man. Contribute to something great."

"And yet ye had no family or woman in your clan? No MacLeod lass? Oft, men see marriage and having bairns as a way to greatness."

Rafe shook his head. "Nay, and I am young and hale. I presumed the Bruce might find a use for my sword."

Her eyes glanced at the broadsword strapped to his back.

"I had a small wooden sword that Kellan had made for me when I was younger," she told him. "Then the men play-fought with me, training me like I was a lad. Nevan was smarter, though. He taught me to use a dirk. He claimed 'twould fit better in my small hand."

She looked down at her pale fingers, a sure sign that she was indeed a lass and not a lad. 'Twas one of the first things Rafe had noticed about her when he was introduced to Bren. Then her eyes flicked up to Rafe.

Well, not to Rafe, he noted. Her gaze seemed directed just past his head. To the handle of his broadsword again.

"Will ye show me how to use a real one?" she asked.

Though 'twas an innocent enough question, a flash of nervous caution flagged in his mind. But it was just showing Brenna his sword. What harm could there be in that?

Rafe stood, his powerful legs moving with ease under the folds of his kilt. He reached his arm to his back and, with a swooshing sound, he withdrew the heavy broadsword that glinted in the sunlight. With his other hand, he reached out to Brenna.

An excited smile split her face, and she grabbed at his hand, scrambling awkwardly in her skirts.

"I should have worn my braies," she mumbled under her breath.

Keeping her hand in his, Rafe led her to the side of the plaid blanket. Then he stood, legs spread shoulder width apart, and held the broadsword in both hands before him.

"Tis a guard stance. 'Tis when ye get your bearings, note the landscape, and size up your opponent. The sword should feel like an extension of your arm. Ye want to try to hold it?"

The sword probably weighed half as much as the lass. That didn't stop Brenna from reaching for it, or stop Rafe from handing it over. When he believed she had a strong grip on the leather-bound handle, he let go of the blade. The tip clunked to the ground with such force it made Rafe cringe.

"Oh, 'tis heavier than it looks," Brenna said as she tried once more to lift the sword with both hands. Rafe bit back a laugh, watching her struggle with the weapon.

"Nay a wooden sword. Here, like this," he said, moving to her back.

He wrapped his arms around hers and, placing his strong grip over her hands, helped her lift the sword from the grass.

That moment was when Rafe realized his mistake. The rounded curve of her buttocks pressed against his groin and thighs, wriggling as she moved in his arms. The feeling of her body against his was more than he could bear. And he lost every last bit of his sense and control.

***

Brenna wasn't certain of Rafe's intentions when he moved behind her to help her clasp the sword in her hands. The way he pressed his chest against her, his strong arms wrapped around her . . .

He had been right, the night before. Her own attentions had been less than noble, and she'd been shocked at her own audacity. What had come over her?

The barn was no place for a man to show his affections for a lass. And from their earlier kisses and heartfelt conversation, Brenna was confident that the man did have an interest in her, in as much as her limited experience could discern. She assured herself 'twas his nobility of spirit that he wouldn't ravish her in the shadowy recesses of a stinking barn.

Dawn, Anne, her uncle, Rafe, they were all correct. Taking Dawn's words to heart, and under the watchful portrait of her mother, Brenna concluded that her time for mourning, for hiding, had to come to an end. With the same force of will as when she became Bren, she threw off that mantle and became Brenna once more. Her new world had far better things to focus on.

And Rafe — he was most of that focus. He'd awakened a life inside her, like the elusive orchid that bursts suddenly into bloom in the summer. Until she had met him, she'd been cast adrift, hiding everything of herself to escape from the world. She'd wallowed in a deep well of self-pity and enjoyed the freedoms of pretending to be Bren for so long, she wasn't sure how to become herself again. Rafe had reopened that world, lighting a fire of passion in her body she didn't know she had.

The more she sought him out, however, the more he seemed to retreat. And her uncle's guards had not made seeking him out easy. She'd had to dodge and sneak around to avoid them. Just today, she'd sent poor Kellan on a fool's errand so she could slip away from the keep unnoticed with Rafe.

And now here she was, in his arms, and her whole body lit up in a lightning storm, crashing, powerful, quivering. 'Twas a series of sensations she hadn't known existed — and it was a welcome change to the absence of any true joy in life that she'd grown accustomed to. Rafe sauntered in that casual way of his, right into her heart.

Brenna wiggled again, adjusting her grip on the sword, and Rafe groaned from deep in his chest, his breath blowing against her hair.

"Show me how to use it," she demanded in a low voice, and he groaned again. If she'd understood how suggestive her words were, she'd didn't let Rafe know. She was a blend of sensuality and innocence, and his body responded with a vengeance.

"Like this." His voice was a ragged whisper against her skin.

He shifted the sword up in her arms, crushing her against his hard chest and thighs. The sword movements became a dance, a seductive series of pressing and thrusting and drove her tighter against Rafe so she felt his every muscle under his tunic and plaid, including the male part of him that bore into her backside.

After a few light swings of the broadsword, Rafe let go with one hand, twisting her in his arms so the sword fell to their sides as she faced him. They panted in rhythm, and Rafe's eyes glanced at her heaving breasts that pulsed against the scooped neckline of her dress. Then his gaze returned to hers, a blue heat that pierced deep into her.

He threw the sword to the ground and clutched both arms around her back, pulling her face up to his.

"Are ye sure ye want this?" he growled.

A flush of fear and desire filled her, and her heart thrummed against her chest. Did she want this? Was she ready to throw off her false identity and be the woman she wanted to be? If she said yes, there was no turning back. This was the moment her life would truly change.

"Aye." Her voice was no more than a whisper.

But it was all he needed. His lips crushed against hers with needy ferocity, claiming her for his own.

***

All else in the world — clans, history, family, and kin — everything fell away as the kiss deepened, tongues touching and retreating. That quivering heat inside Brenna grew to a crescendo, pulsing in her head, her arms, her stomach, and lower in her woman's mound. It was everything and nothing. and she was mindlessly limp.

Rafe clenched his iron-like arms around her, snuggling her against the breadth of his chest. Her heart pounded in an erratic vibration, and the sheer shock of their bold acts buzzed through her body.

He knelt, lowering her with him so they sat on her plaid, his hands holding her upright against him, and his lips never left her skin. He tugged gently at her gown and exposed the creamy flesh of her shoulder, and seared her skin with kisses down her neck, igniting a burning low in her belly.

Brenna's senses reeled, and her body spun out of control. There was no other sensation for her but for the touch of his lips on her skin. Is this what it was to love? To share loving with a man? What power and excitement!

She gasped when his hands slipped under her skirts, a jolt of nervous ache shivering up her thighs. He stopped and lifted his head, his brow crinkled in alarm.

"Did I hurt ye? Do ye want me to stop?"

And he would stop. If she said aye, he would immediately release her and escort her home in the most noble manner. But his body, matching her own, screamed and begged that she didn't.

"Nay. I want ye, Rafe. I've never felt anything like this, like what I feel when I'm with ye."

Rafe shook his head, her words clenching at his heart.

"Or I for ye. I should walk away. I should do the virtuous thing and leave ye. Ye are naught but a lass. I should no' overstep."

He hated saying the words. Giving her pause to reject him when he wanted her, needed her so desperately. She had said she'd not felt anything like what they seemed to share, and it was the same for Rafe. This loving was mad. Chaotic. Impossible. Yet it was also everything he had ever wanted.

She laid a dainty hand on his cheek.

"I said, I want ye."

There it was, that willfulness that had served her so well was serving her again. And Rafe was at her mercy. He could only obey her command, a man possessed.

He was possessed by her. *He loved her.*

Her soft breath fanned his face, and he captured her lips in a delicate kiss that claimed her as his own. Brenna's hand clenched at his jaw, holding the kiss.

Wiggling under his embrace, she slid the wide neckline off her slender shoulder where it fell to the chain girdle at her hips. The swell of her breasts, smooth and pink-tipped and a wondrous sight invited his kisses, and he grazed his lips across a gentle slope. She gasped again, but this time held his head in place so he couldn't pull away.

Rafe pressed her back into the tartan, and his hand moved under her skirts again. Her thighs quivered but opened slightly, permitting his fingers to explore the dewy skin of her thighs and the crest of her womanhood.

Another gasp, this one wide-eyed. Rafe took that moment to withdraw and pull his tunic over his head. Those wide eyes flashed with excitement as he studied her, searching for any sign of fear or refusal. Instead, her burning amber gaze danced over his chest, studying his chiseled muscles and swirls of black hair with the same intensity. Then he unclasped his belt and let the heavy plaid fabric fall from his sculpted body, and those eyes glinted more.

She didn't flinch or recoil, as an unexperienced lass might, and he raised an eyebrow in question. Brenna flashed him a smirk.

"'Tis larger, close up."

Rafe started, instinctively moving his hands to his groin.

"Wait, what?"

She giggled as she looked up at him, and his eyes dropped to her breasts that shook with her.

"I saw ye. All those days ago, when ye came to the loch for a swim and learned about me? I left, but no' right away. I watched ye swim first."

Her side-grin was wicked as she continued to stare, and Rafe guffawed at her audacity. She might have seemed the fragile flower, but years of being brash in a lad's clothes had bred deep into her. Brenna was far more brazen than Rafe ever imagined.

Rafe didn't move. He remained on his knees, letting her look his fill. He could be as brazen as this little lass.

"Ye got to see it. Are ye going to touch it?"

She hadn't expected that, as her hand flew to her mouth in scandal. Rafe chuckled again.

Then her hand left her mouth, and she grasped the length of him, a gentle, inexperienced touch.

A low grumble emanated from Rafe.

"Ye can squeeze it a bit."

In a bold move, she did just that, and the grip of her hand forced a frantic groan from his lips.

"Ooch, lass. I want to be slow for ye, for your first time. I dinna ken if I can control myself," he told her in a husky voice. He didn't know if she knew what to expect, and he wanted to be honest with her. "There can be some pain for a lassie's first time."

She removed her hand, then squirmed under his gaze, slipping the gown the rest of the way off her body. Brenna lay beneath him in her bare perfection. Another uncontrollable groan escaped him.

"Then love me as ye best know how, and I will love ye the best I know how. I'm certain our bodies will meet in the middle."

Rafe leaned down and covered her body with his. His skin was hot against hers, his chest and hips grazing hers. The hairs on his chest tingled against her taut nipples.

"Ye are too wise by half, Brenna."

Then he kissed her again, shifting his legs between hers. She opened them to allow him access. If she had any fear or hesitation, she didn't show it. Every part of her wanted him, was inviting him, and he accepted that invitation.

Brenna shook with anxious tension — the passion coursing through her was one of nervous excitement, but she wanted this man too much to care. And as his hands and lips seared her skin with his touches and kisses, all thoughts and fear fled. 'Twas only her and Rafe, here under the brilliant sky.

When the tip of his member pressed in, he moved gradually, with careful exactness, and she gasped again, this time in pain, as he fully entered her. But his hands and lips didn't stop, and when her breathing changed from the shock of being filled to the desire of being one with Rafe, he began to move in slow, delicate thrusts.

Her body melted against him as he moved, this strange thrill of his hardness inside her, of being complete, and she clasped her hands at his back, needing more of him. Awe filled her again at how her body responded to him, welcoming him, clenching at him, and as his gyrations intensified, so did the burning vibration in her core.

Rafe panted and thrusted over her, his own passions consuming him. In a sudden rush, he threw his head back and called to her, chanting "Brenna!" over and over as he spilled into her.

Their act of raw possession was over, and he collapsed atop her breasts, his panting matching her own. The feeling of joining, of the satisfaction he gave her lingered, and Brenna wanted that sensation to endure.

They lay under that sky the same shade as Rafe's eyes, entwined as one, their lives forever changed and as entwined as their bodies. Brenna needed this man by her side. She clung to him as his breathing slowed, as if she feared she might lose him that very moment.

Rafe sensed the change in her embrace and tightened his own arms.

He wasn't going anywhere.

***

"Are ye well?" he finally asked, breaking the still of the day. Only the gentle lapping of the loch against the grassy banks broke the silence.

"Aye. Better than I thought I'd be. Truly I did no' ken what to expect."

He lifted himself from her, gazing at her with smoldering intensity.

"Ye dinna regret it, do ye?"

Her clear brow furrowed. "Nay. Do ye?"

Rafe shook his head, but his lips pulled taut.

"I should. God save me, I feel as if I have taken advantage of ye. I fear this was too sudden for ye. That ye dinna know me well enough to take this step. Yet I dinna regret it. God save me, no' at all."

His tender eyes searched hers. "I canna help it. I've fallen in – "

She placed her finger on his lips to stop him. A slight smile tugged at Brenna's mouth.

"I believe I feel the same," she whispered. "If anything, I took advantage of ye. And it's no' as sudden as it might seem. My uncle, my kin, have been encouraging me to shed my costumes and assume my role in the clan. Perchance I just needed the right inducement."

"Ooch, and that's me?" Rafe's face softened. "I'm inducement?"

"And a good inducement ye are," she teased, ruffling his sun-kissed dark locks.

Chapter Twelve: When We Learn the Truth

RAFE WAS IN A STATE of shock as they walked back to the keep. He'd had a moment, A moment with this woman contrary to anything he'd experienced in his life. The one woman he should *not* have had in his bed.

He'd had women. Many women. Wanton lasses in the shadows, maids in rented rooms or in furtive couplings behind a croft.

But those had been one-offs, singular moments he'd not given another thought. Numerous women who blended facelessly across his past.

Today, with this woman, was life changing.

Brenna.

His time with her was anything but momentary. She was anything but faceless. Her fragility that paired with a subtle will . . . her manner of getting her way even when it seemed unachievable. The dichotomy of the lass — she who wanted to live as a lad but emerged as a sultry woman, she who was fragile and strong, she who was docile and commanding. How did she manage to hold both heaven and hell in her hand?

Heaven. The time Rafe had spent with her marked his mind and his heart. Brenna haunted his dreams and his loins. He pined for her — yearned for her. Rafe had never known how powerful of an emotion 'twas to pine for a woman. Each kiss reached past his lips to clutch at his heart. He could be a different man, a better man, because of her. And he longed to be that man.

Even before their loving by the loch, he'd fallen for her. Forget going to find the Bruce, he considered the possibility of settling into clan Fraser with this dainty, intense lass.

Hell. That dream would never come to fruition. The MacKay clan had traumatized the Fraser clan, and if he were to wed this lass that held his heart with such conviction, he'd have to give his true name. Then Brenna, and her entire clan, would reject him when they learned of his heritage.

Rafe had come far — he'd done much for this clan. He could hope that his MacKay kinship might be forgiven and forgotten. But Highlanders have long memories. As much as he hated the prospect, especially after that perfect interlude with Brenna, he must leave.

Riding and fighting for the Bruce was the only opportunity he had of clearing his name, showing he was worthy regardless of what clan he came from, and then mayhap, *mayhap*, he might win Brenna's hand. 'Twas the only chance he had.

"Rafe, what do ye think?" Brenna interrupted his distracted thoughts.

"My apologies, love. I was woolgathering. What did ye ask?"

"We're here."

Brenna pointed to the low-walled enclosure adjacent to the church. The graveyard. A few lone stones had sunk deep into the grass and were overgrown. Several markers, however, stood tall against the overgrowth. Rounded standing stones with Celtic knots engraved on them. Brenna led him closer to those stones.

A sickening sensation clenched at Rafe's chest. No good news came from a graveyard.

Brenna knelt before those two tall stones. A first name and a date were etched onto each.

Braden 1301. Maud 1301.

Her beloved brother. Her admired mother.

The clenching in Rafe's chest worsened, and his head spun with an unpleasant levity. Nevertheless, he knelt next to Brenna, his eyes fixated on the stones.

Such heartache. Such loss. Then with her father's illness on top of all that. If he could take on her pain to himself, permit her to walk in a world free of such suffering, he would take that on his own broad shoulders without question.

Her loss made Rafe's departure from his clan seem so insignificant. What was it to choose to walk away from one's clan compared to having everything you know and love ripped away as a child?

And knowing he was lying to her, even as they knelt in front of her mother's and her brother's graves, tightened Rafe's chest pain.

It canna get worse than this.

"Six years." Brenna's light voice broke through the solemnness of the cemetery. "Some days I can no' believe 'tis been so long. Some days it seems like yesterday."

Rafe remained silent as Brenna found her voice. He slipped his arm around her waist to support her, and she settled comfortably against him.

"Has anyone told ye the story of what happened? Why it sent us into such a state?"

"I've heard rumblings, no more. I imagine the death of a brother and mother so suddenly might send anyone into such a state," he answered honestly.

"Aye," Brenna agreed. "But it didn't have to happen. That is the worst. Like other nearby smaller clans, the MacKays oft found sport in reiving our cattle, harassing our lasses, stealing foodstuffs or ironworks. All manner of minor offenses."

The mention of the MacKays caused Rafe to stiffen and a chasm in his chest to form. He'd known that his clan had been the cause of much animosity among the Highland clans, particularly with the Frasers. Now his hair stood on end with the connection to Brenna's brother.

Nay . . .

"My brother and several other lads decided to retrieve the cattle. So foolish. 'Twas three cows. Three meager Highland bessies. They came upon the MacKays in a clearing near the MacKay's land. We dinna ken the details, but a fight ensued, and one MacKay pulled a dirk and stabbed my brother in the back."

A lone tear rolled down Brenna's cheek, and she wiped it away with her sleeve. Rafe didn't breathe.

"The wound didn't bleed overmuch. My mother and her maid took to Braden's aid, sent for the surgeon. My uncle sent for the priest. The blood wasn't pouring out, but he was bleeding on the inside, the surgeon later told us. He died in my mother's arms as she tried to staunch the wound. She screamed the whole time, begging my brother to live, my father to help her, the surgeon to do something, God to intervene. None of that happened."

"Did someone tell you this?" Rafe asked, even though in his heart he knew differently. Brenna must have watched this horrific scene unfold.

Brenna shook her head.

"Nay. No one saw me in the corner of the room. Until Dawn entered to help calm my mother. She noticed me cowering behind the trunk. She told me I was pale, stricken, mute. She tried to remove me from the chambers, but I fought to stay, clinging to the trunk. Eventually my uncle removed it to my room. I didn't stay. First, I snuck into my mother's chambers. Then she died. I snuck

170

back into my brother's chambers, and 'tis were I remained. I didn't want to leave the chambers, so I dressed in my brother's clothes as a way to stay with him, to remain in his room. 'Tis nonsensical, I ken, but it made sense to a lost, twelve-year-old lassie."

The next words tasted of dirt and decay in his mouth.

"And your mother?"

Brenna swallowed hard.

"They say heartache. 'Twas Belladonna."

Rafe's chest exploded. At least, that what it felt like — as though 'twas filled with vitriol and ignited. To take one's life was an unforgivable mortal sin.

And the death of Brenna's brother wasn't an accident. Wasn't of his own accord. 'Twas a direct result of the MacKays. They killed the lad, and because of that, Maud killed herself. And her father descended into a mysterious illness in his grief.

The death of both and her father's health were laid at the feet of the MacKays.

Rafe's clan.

He'd known the lass's full story would be gut-wrenching — death is rarely pleasant.

But to learn the truth, to know that his own men were responsible. Men he sat with for meals, hunted with, drank with.

And he had just coupled with Brenna. Admitted his love for her. Wanted to make certain he could share his life with her.

She had lain with a man of the clan who killed her brother and mother.

Dear God . . .

Rafe would be fortunate to leave with his head still on his shoulders if the Frasers learned his true identity. The only bright spot, if it could be called that, was that he wasn't with those MacKays who victimized Braden. For that, Rafe was eternally grateful.

Regardless, if he were present or not, any chance he'd had of returning from the Bruce to wed this woman was gone.

He pasted a fake smile on his face, crushing Brenna's delicate shoulders in his embrace.

"Thank ye for sharing this with me. My heart grieves for ye and your family."

Brenna tried to shrug it off, masking her pain.

"'Tis six years past. Time to move on. But the wound is yet raw at times."

"As it should be. We never fully recover from the death of a loved one. It fades, like a bruise, yet remains. And if we press it, touch it the wrong way, 'twill pain us the same as a fresh wound."

"Do ye feel the same for your mother?"

Rafe sighed. 'Twas impossible to compare his never knowing his mother to Brenna's loss. He had to appreciate Brenna's consideration of his loss amid her own heartache.

"'Tis different, I think," he said as he rose and clasped Brenna's elbow to help her stand. "Rather the pain is never having known her. Since I don't know my mother, 'tis no sense of loss in the same way as you feel."

Brenna rubbed at her face to chase away her emotions and find joy again. Under Rafe's gentle gaze, happiness bubbled up easily. The delight he brought her, the excitement that filled her whenever she saw him forced the pain into a small box she could lock away.

"Shall we finish our journey home?" she asked.

"We will need to discuss today," Rafe responded.

He'd taken her virginity, made her a woman, spoke loving promises to her — when he

left for the Bruce, 'twould appear he as though he was abandoning her. He must tell Brenna soon of his goal of joining the Bruce to prove himself worthy.

She may despise his leaving, hate him for loving her and leaving her behind, but if they handfast and he vowed to return, perchance 'twould temper the agony of his departure.

And he had to do all this under the guise of being a MacLeod. 'Twas the only option he had left.

He would be a MacLeod the rest of his life if it meant having Brenna by his side.

"Aye. but we can discuss it later. Let us sup together. I'll find my bed tonight, and in the morn, we will consider our future together. But not yet."

A light smile passed Rafe's lips. She'd said, "our future." Mayhap he could have the happy ending he craved, and Brenna deserved.

They had reached the wall of the Fraser keep. Rafe swept Brenna into his arms, eliciting a surprising squeal from the lass, and kissed her with every promise of their life together. His hands got lost in her short hair, and she pulled on his hips with her dainty fingers. They clung to each other as a breakwater against a raging sea, only their love for each other keeping them from drowning in the world.

"Then I will wait until the morn to announce our handfast," he promised breathlessly, and kissed her again.

Though he desperately wanted that vow to be true, it tasted sourly of a lie on his lips.

***

Dorcas was cleaning the men's space behind the main hall. Too often, Fraser warriors found their sleep after a night of drinking, and the room was oft neglected.

And it stank. If it weren't cleaned regularly, the odor permeated the wall and entered the hall. No one, least of all the kitchen maids, wanted to endure that smell as they prepared meals, ate, or conferenced.

Her first job was to set the rogue items on their respective sleeping pallets. A loose plaid here, a scabbard there, a dirk left behind as the warriors headed out to their work or their patrols. Only then could Dorcas begin emptying the piss pot in the corner and sweeping the floors.

She had picked up most of the misplaced items when a discarded dirk caught her eye, half buried under the plaids on a pallet. She slipped it from its hiding spot and was ready to toss it onto the blankets when an emblem made her pause. That and a strip of bright green and blue plaid. Nay Fraser tartan. The emblem was of a hand clutching a dirk. Nay the Fraser thistles, or even the MacLeod Highland bull.

MacKay plaid. MacKay emblem.

Dorcas didn't know whose pallet hid the dirk, but she knew only one man who should have any belongings not of the Fraser clan.

A man who wasn't a Fraser.

A man who claimed to be a MacLeod.

But why would a MacLeod have a MacKay knife?

She made to lay the dirk on the pallet, then yanked her hand back. Someone must be informed about this. She needed to tell someone. The Laird? Nay, he was sick. Robert? What if she were wrong or overreacting? Dawn?

Aye, sensible, fair Dawn. She always knew what best to do.

Sticking the dirk into the pinned-up fold of her apron, she continued her chores in the room. She decided to show Dawn the knife after they cleaned up from supper.

Chapter Thirteen: Identities Revealed

AN IRATE KELLAN met Rafe and Brenna when they entered the yard. If Robert learned the lass managed to elude Kellan again, the Laird's brother would have his hide in retribution.

"Where have ye been, lass?" he demanded, yanking her arm to drag Brenna away from Rafe. Kellan cut a judgmental eye at the MacLeod man. He knew what young men were up to when left alone with comely lassies.

"I took Rafe to the cemetery," Brenna gave Kellan a half-truth. "I wanted to share with him why I dressed as a lad when he first met me."

Kellan's hard face grew more terse. The idea of sharing any private information about the Frasers of Broch Invershin didn't sit well with Kellan. Neither did the idea that Brenna had been alone with the MacLeod, cemetery or no.

"Weel, come away. Your uncle has need of ye, and I have need of Rafe. We must retrieve some cattle."

Brenna pursed her lips but didn't argue. She sent a quick, soft glance at Rafe, who bowed his head imperceptibly. Her skirts caught around her legs as she raced up the stone steps to the main hall.

"Are ye ready to ride?" Kellan asked, his voice as hard as his visage. "Nevan is joining us with several other Frasers. We could use your size as we retrieve our possessions."

He didn't give Rafe the chance to answer. Grabbing at Rafe's threadbare tunic, Kellan dragged him toward the stables, where Nevan and the other Fraser warriors were preparing for their task.

***

Fuming inwardly, Rafe mounted a borrowed steed and followed the men as they galloped from the keep to the north west. So much for trying to leave unnoticed again. It seemed the fates were determined to keep him on the Fraser land.

All too soon, Rafe recognized the shift in the land again, from the stonier base of the mountain past the wide glens.

Oh no. No no no.

How could such a thing be possible? What foul timing was this? Could the day get any worse?

They didn't even need to reach the outskirts of the MacKay lands before they encountered a force of men, MacKay men, whose job it was to thieve from local clans.

The clash near the glen happened without hesitation. Kellan and Nevan didn't halt their horses, instead launching themselves from their saddles at the MacKays who'd begun to make camp. The MacKays reacted as swiftly, drawing their swords in defense.

A moment of indecision raged through Rafe before he reacted. And his movements were motivated by one thing only — Brenna. His old MacKay kin would just as soon ravish the women of the Fraser clan, Brenna included, as steal food or cattle. And if the MacKays had resumed their outlaw behavior with the Frasers, their crimes would only get worse. Rafe reached over his head to extract his broadsword in one smooth motion. He vowed to defend Brenna and her land, no matter what. MacKay kin or not.

Rafe was acquainted with two of the men. Unlike the Frasers, Rafe didn't rush in — he hung back, catching the sword tip of a man with whom he was unfamiliar. The MacKay man parried well but had not trained in a while and it showed. Rafe thrust and feinted, then dropped low to slit the man's gullet. He collapsed to the ground with a gurgle and a splay of blood.

Rafe believed he might have experienced a manner of guilt or shame in killing a MacKay warrior, but he didn't. Moving closer to the Frasers, Rafe stopped short when he heard his name. And he wasn't the only one who stopped.

"Rafe? 'Tis ye? Have ye been with the Frasers this whole time? Why are ye here?"

Rafe's mind spun. Gritting his teeth, he lunged with deft speed at the man who recognized him. The MacKay warrior was caught unaware and fell hard with a jab at his chest.

When Rafe circled around to see how the Frasers fared, Nevan stood several feet away, his sword hanging at his side, his face contorted with angry confusion.

Nevan didn't say anything. He waited until the Frasers dispatched the remainder of the MacKays, then Nevan mounted his horse. He said nothing — he didn't have to. The accusations in his eyes said it all.

The ground wept in the blood of MacKays, and once the offending clan was ravaged, Nevan commanded the men to mount up and return home. Their work in stopping the MacKays from damaging the Frasers had been completed with deadly efficiency. They might not have retrieved their cattle, but their message had been sent. After the life-changing attack six years ago, the Frasers took no chances when it came to the MacKays.

Nevan rode next to Kellan, their low voices deep in conversation. Kellan's head flicked over his shoulder toward the rear of the riding party, in Rafe's direction, but he didn't look at Rafe full on.

The discovery of Rafe's MacKay identity was not going to be forgiven, not knowing what he did about the Laird and his family. Rafe was honestly shocked Nevan hadn't slain him where they stood in the glen.

As much as Rafe hated himself for it, he vowed to gather his belongings secretly and leave, flee in truth. And he must do it without a word to Brenna. He couldn't bring himself to look at her lovely, innocent face and admit the horror of his deception and what he had done with her under his guise. She would be devastated.

In a rash moment, he wondered if Brenna might leave with him, run away to join the Bruce. He could beg her to come with him before she learned the truth of who he was.

He shook his head as he rode. Nay, 'twas a childish thought — a fantasy. Run away together — that was not a future he was destined to have. His only choice was to leave Brenna, and with her his heart, behind.

***

Once they returned to Broch Invershin, Rafe tossed the reins of the horse around a post at the front of the keep instead of stabling his steed. The horse pawed at the thin grass, searching for a juicy patch to nibble while Rafe leapt up the steps to the main hall.

"Rafe! *MacLeod.*" Nevan's voice was unmistakable — the man's tone held a note of ridicule. Rafe paused mid-step, one leg upraised in a comical pose, and glanced behind him.

Nevan stood with Kellan and his Highlanders, a wall of Frasers, with arms crossed and anger emanating like a cloud. Rafe hung his head and cringed. He would not be leaving this night. If ever.

"Ye need to come with us. We will see what the Laird's brother wants to do with ye."

Rafe stood tall, his jaw set. Confrontation was one option — to fight his way past the men. Yet, these same men had just killed off a MacKay raiding party, and blood lust was a powerful force. They'd never let him pass with his life.

His best chance was to go with them, plead his case with Robert or the ill Laird he'd never met, and pray they chose to release him into the graces of the Bruce.

Otherwise, he'd end up with his head on a pike for his deception.

And if they learned he'd lain with Brenna, who knew what other body parts would end up impaled on a stick? A shudder rang through Rafe and rattled his bones.

Nevan grabbed his arms as Kellan yanked his broadsword off his back. Forcing Rafe's hands immobile, they led him to a weathered croft that was missing part of the thatched roof. At least it wasn't a dungeon.

One of the Fraser men held a length of rope, and they bound him to an iron link set into the wall of the croft. Giving Rafe an angry glare, Nevan and his men left, slamming the door and leaving Rafe to consider the misery of his life choices.

The only beacon of light in his sudden change in circumstance was Brenna. He tried to keep her face before his eyes, to think of her and not of his impending death. And he prayed that learning of his subterfuge would not set her running back to her brother's clothes and her false identity. She was a stunning woman who deserved to live the fullness of that life. She deserved better than him.

Rafe had sought to rise above his station in life, tried to be someone he wasn't, and he lost everything in doing so. He hung his head, lost in his somber thoughts.

Chapter Fourteen: Damning Evidence

DORCAS BROUGHT THE KNIFE to Dawn, who turned it over and over in the firelight as Dorcas explained where she found it. Dawn tried to question Dorcas, to give the MacLeod man the benefit of her doubt. The dirk, with its plaid and emblem, was too damning. There was no other reason Dawn could conceive for why the man would own a MacKay item.

If he wasn't a MacKay, then at the very least, he stole it. The man was a thief then.

And he was trying to thieve Brenna's heart.

The villain.

"Do we tell Brenna?" Dorcas asked with hesitancy.

The clansmen and women effortlessly fell back into calling her Brenna. They had accepted her return with zeal, just as Dawn had assumed they would. Bren had not stuck well as it was, so it was easy to go back.

Dawn wanted to throw the knife in the fire, pretend it was never found. She too often saw the good in people – it had not entered her head that the handsome MacLeod might hide an odious nature. When Brenna learned the truth, 'twould destroy the lass, and she would surely backslide, lose her identity again. And Dawn was the one who encouraged her to follow her heart with Rafe. *More the fool, me*, Dawn thought bitterly.

"I believe we must," Dawn admitted with a heavy heart. "She will need to make some decisions. I believe the lass is in love with the man. This, regardless of the truth behind it, must be made known so she can ask him."

The last part of Dawn's statement was more of a question, and Dorcas nodded in agreement. Once they brought the evidence to Brenna, then they could decide when and how to bring what they knew to Robert.

"Do ye want me to come with ye when you tell her?" Dorcas offered.

Such a kind soul, Dawn said to herself. She shook her blonde locks.

"Nay. I shall do it."

Relief flooded Dorcas's face, and she bowed and stepped away, leaving Dawn alone with the knife.

Dawn twisted it over in her hand again, laboring for the best way to tell Brenna something was amiss with her new man. Sighing reservedly, Dawn slipped the dirk into her skirts and grabbed a torch before climbing the stairs to Brenna's chambers. She dragged her feet, cursing her task.

She tucked the torch into the sconce outside Brenna's door and knocked. A bright-eyed Brenna opened the door. Dawn recognized the exuberant expression on the lassie's face. She and her man were in love and had expressed it with each other — Dawn had no doubt.

Her heart sunk in her chest. That was going to make her task even more difficult.

"Dawn! What a pleasure. Please come in. Do ye need something from me?" Brenna swept to the side and Dawn entered, appreciating the new look to Braden's old rooms. So much change, acceptance, and restoration for Brenna, as evidenced by this chamber, by the very gown the lassie wore, and Dawn was here to rip it all away. She took a deep breath before starting.

"Nay, but I do need to have a conversation with ye. 'Tis of import."

Her voice was low, but Brenna didn't hear the distress. 'Twas obvious she was too caught up in her thoughts to pay attention.

"Brenna, please sit with me."

Dawn perched on the edge of the bedding and patted the space next to her. Brenna placed the plaid over her chair and joined Dawn on the bed. She still had that satisfied look on her face.

And Dawn was complicit in that. Too often she'd kept Brenna's escapades from her guards, misdirecting Nevan or Kellan so Brenna might have her privacy. Any lass needs her privacy, even if she dressed as a lad. These past few days had been no different; only this time, Brenna's escapades had involved Rafe.

From Brenna's shining face, Dawn well understood that Rafe was more than just a passing fancy. Dawn's heart pounded in her chest. If Brenna had fallen in love with the stranger, or worse, had coupled with the man, then this news would devastate her. Another loss was the last thing Brenna needed. Dawn braced herself.

"Why do ye appear so serious, Dawn? Is something amiss?" A cloud crossed Brenna's shining face. "Is it Father?"

"Nay, no' your father," Dawn said hurriedly, "but something may well be amiss. Brenna, how much do ye ken of Rafe MacLeod?"

Brenna stiffened at the question.

"He's an only child. His mother died when he was a wee bairn, and his father was a sad drunk who died a while ago."

"And how did ye end up bringing him to Broch Invershin?"

"He was traveling to join the Bruce. He missed leaving with other MacLeod men and wasn't certain of where the Bruce was. We have men returning soon, or so I'd heard Duncan say, and thought he might reside with us, learn of the Bruce's location from our warriors, and join the Bruce then."

"Did he say why he was delayed? Why he left his clan alone?"

Brenna's face twisted with bewilderment at Dawn's query. Dawn made it seem Rafe had separate motives for leaving his clan.

"Why are ye asking, Dawn?"

Brenna's voice was measured as she steeled herself for what Dawn struggled to say. She had finally come out of her shell, and she had fallen hard, too hard, for the wickedly handsome, raven-haired MacLeod warrior. With his bright eyes and easy smile and interest in Brenna, Dawn knew Brenna was lost within days of meeting him.

And Brenna held tight to that attachment as she left her mourning behind. Without Rafe, it might have been years before she resumed her position as Brenna, daughter of the Laird, if at all. If something was amiss with Rafe, Brenna might not handle the news.

Dawn saw all these emotions painted on Brenna's innocent features. She tempered her thoughts and withdrew her hand from her kirtle.

The dirk glinted in the setting sunlight, casting a long shadow over Dawn's stained skirts. The strip of rich blue and green fabric draped over her arm. Brenna said nothing, staring at the weapon.

She didn't touch it, or even reach for it. The icon of the hand on the handle was bold and easy to see, and Brenna pulled away, shivering in fear over the tiny knife.

"What are ye showing me?" she asked Dawn in a nervous voice.

Dawn's heart broke at that sound.

"Dorcas found it today, whilst Rafe was out. She was cleaning the sleeping quarters behind the hall. 'Twas under Rafe's pallet."

"And what do ye think it means?"

Brenna's wide eyes flicked with apprehension from the dirk to Dawn and back.

"I dinna ken. Ye see 'tis a MacKay dirk, the emblem. And MacKay plaid."

"And Dorcas found this with Rafe's belongings? Why does he have a MacKay dirk?"

Oh, ye innocent lassie, Dawn thought.

"There could be many reasons. Mayhap he found it," Dawn started to say, trying to keep her tone light and encouraging. But Brenna needed to know the other possible reasons why the man had the knife. "Or, mayhap he stole it. When ye were at the Inn or before that. Or mayhap . . ."

Dawn was desperate to give Brenna another reason, but her voice trailed off, and Brenna's face searched hers.

"Or mayhap what, Dawn?"

She's going to make me say it. She canna bring herself to admit it.

"Or mayhap he's no' a MacLeod."

Brenna blinked several times, trying to stomach Dawn's implication.

"No' a MacLeod? But then what —?" Her pale hand flew to her face. "Nay," she whispered. Gooseflesh covered Brenna's skin.

"Brenna —" Dawn set the dirk aside and reached for the distraught lass.

"Nay," she said again, with more force. "Ye canna be suggesting Rafe is a MacKay. 'Tis no' possible!"

"How is it no' possible? If ye were traveling alone, southward, crossing clan lands that your own kin had abused, wouldn't ye want to hide who you are? Ye of all should know —"

"'Tis no' possible!" Brenna jumped to her feet and paced the room. Dawn joined her, trying to calm Brenna's fretting. "He canna have lied to me, Dawn. He said he loved me. He said . . ."

She didn't finish. Brenna crumpled to the floor in familiar tears, the pain of this potentially devastating news overwhelming her. Dawn wrapped her arms around Brenna's head, cooing and patting her hair.

"We dinna ken for sure, Brenna. He could have found or stole the dirk. We must ask him."

"Ask him?" Brenna cried into Dawn's skirts. "I dinna want to see him!"

"We dinna ken if he is lying about his clan. Verily, the only way to ken is to ask him. Once ye have gathered yourself, we will search out Nevan and have him escort us to ask Rafe. Sufficient unto the day is the evil therein. Dinna expect the worst, yet."

Brenna wiped her eyes with the hem of her gown. Dawn spoke the truth.

"Aye. No' yet."

***

Brenna felt so agonizingly alone. In her grief, she turned to the one person she felt she had left, mindless though he might be. Her father.

Dawn escorted her to the Laird's door, and after knocking for the attending maid, she stepped to the side to let Brenna have her time with her father.

Anne opened the door, giving Brenna a welcoming smile.

"Och, in a dress! Yesterday ye were in braies! What a pleasant surprise. Do I still call ye Bren then? Or can I call ye Brenna again?"

A slight smile snuck out from Brenna's lips. Anne's positivity was a force to be reckoned with. 'Twas difficult to feel low when that woman was around. No wonder she was such a good match to attend her father. And her uncle.

"Brenna, please Anne. I'm trying to come back to myself. I canna hide my whole life, can I?" Brenna told her with a conviction she didn't truly feel.

"Nay. Ye need to be your true self — and whether that's in braies or in a kirtle, 'tis of small consequence. Your father just wants ye to be whoever makes ye happiest."

Ahh, so refreshing after the judgment of wearing a lad's clothes, then the fear of judgment in returning to dresses as she came out of mourning.

And truthfully, 'twas a sight easier to ride a horse in braies. Wearing gowns didn't mean she had abandoned the other clothes completely.

"Thank ye, Anne. I appreciate that. Is my father well enough for a visit?"

"Ye can visit anytime, lassie. That ye ken. Well or no'. Even on his worst days, it does his heart good to see ye."

Even if he does no' know me. Brenna nodded and entered, approaching her father's bed with caution. Every time she saw him, her heart broke a little more, and she wanted to run away and hide in her brother's clothes again.

The powerful warrior once had a long, thick swath of rich earthy hair, dancing eyes, and open arms, ready to sweep her up in a strong embrace. He'd swing her around so her feet flew out, and she'd screech with laughter.

All she had were those memories. The man in bed before her was a shadow of the warrior she called father. And now, when she needed those strong arms the most, she would be fortunate if he could even recall her name.

His distracted gaze noted Brenna as she stepped closer to the bed. His face lit up with joy.

"Maud! Maud! I have missed ye, lassie mine! Why have I no' seen ye? I have missed ye so much."

Brenna broke at her father's words. She glanced at her gown — 'twas her mother's. And with Brenna's bronzed coloring, she knew from the portrait that presently hung in her room how much she resembled her mother.

Her father didn't see her. He only saw his long-gone beloved Maud.

But her mother didn't need him. Brenna did. Especially now.

And he didn't know her at all.

"Hello, Father. It's not Maud. It's your daughter, Brenna."

Kevin squinted at Brenna, as though trying to see her through a thick fog.

"Nay, my Brenna, she wears a laddie's tunic and braies. Maud, I always loved ye in those wood-like colors. Ye resemble a woodland sprite." Kevin grinned widely at the loose memories of his wife.

Brenna looked to Anne for help, but the maid only shrugged.

"Do your best. He may remember ye after a bit, or he may continue to see Maud," Anne advised.

"I know I look like Maud, Father. That's because I'm her daughter. Brenna. I'm Maud's daughter."

"Nay, Brenna likes to be called Bren and chase around her guards. She's still little. Oh Maud, ye are so beautiful. I must have forgotten how striking your beauty is."

'Twas no use. Her father's mind, so tenuous for so long, seemed to have cracked completely. Just as she was starting to come out of her pain, find someone to start the second part of her life with her, more loss crashed against her in a wave.

He didn't see her. He only saw her poor dead mother.

Brenna's shoulders sagged, and Anne was there to put a loving arm around her shaky shoulders.

"Dinna let it get to ye. He may recall ye tomorrow."

"Will he ever get better?" Brenna asked, but she already knew the answer to that question.

Anne shook her head. "Nay, lassie. He will only grow worse until heaven claims his sad soul."

Brenna cast a long, mournful look at her father.

"Have ye told my uncle how bad he is?"

"He's visited your father, but I believe he knows the full extent. The Laird no' recognizing his own daughter . . ."

"Aye. I understand. I think 'tis time for my uncle and I to accept that truth. Thank ye, Anne, for all ye do for my father."

"Of course, lassie. And dinna forget what I told ye. Your father would no' want ye to waste away in mourning and pain. No' for your mother or brother, and no' for him. The greatest gift ye can give your father is to be happy, whether he knows it or no."

***

Nevan found Duncan when he returned from the MacLeods, grabbing the reins as Duncan dismounted. They shared grim expressions.

"Duncan, I must have a word with ye."

"I must meet with Robert straight away. Can it wait?" Duncan faced Nevan with severity. "And please tell me ye have kept a fierce eye on Brenna around that MacLeod fool."

Nevan chewed his lip, knowing the lass had been out of his sight for much of the day as he dealt with duties to the keep and the MacKays.

"Nay, but Rafe was with me this afternoon. 'Tis that man I need to discuss with ye."

Duncan's tight face hardened even more.

"He's the reason I must find Robert. What is your concern with Rafe?"

"He's no' a MacLeod. He's a MacKay."

His worst presumption had been correct, and fury exploded in Duncan like a vitriol-fed pyre. Unable to control it, he spun sharply and punched the daubed wall of the stables, which crumbled under his knuckles.

"I have just come back from the MacLeods. My cousin and his Laird did no' ken the man. How did ye learn he's a MacKay?"

"That vile clan reived from us again. I had Rafe accompany us when we tracked the raiding party to eliminate them. One of their men called him by name."

The rage bubbled again, and Duncan assaulted the now-crumbling wall over and over. Once a large hole was well entrenched and his knuckles were bloody, Duncan paused, panting to catch his breath and control his rage.

"And we let that lying cretin near Brenna. Into our clan. We failed horribly, Nevan. Davis!" Duncan hollered across the stables to a hardy stable lad. "Repair the wall. Nevan and I have a duty to attend."

The enraged giants made for the main hall and found Robert in the Laird's study. They burst in with no greeting, slamming the chamber door wide.

"What is this?" Robert jumped at their entry.

"Robert, we have a problem."

"The MacLeod man?"

Duncan and Nevan exchanged a hard gaze.

"I think ye mean the MacKay man," Duncan spat out.

Robert was an immense man, a warrior who'd seen battles and fought and won when he'd been outnumbered. He was a man who wielded his claymore as a child wielded a toy. Yet, he stumbled back into the chair, pale and weak, clutching at his tunic.

The man who he welcomed to his clan, opened his home to, who had befriended his dear Brenna, was a MacKay? 'Twas worse than he imagined.

The pounding in his head crushed his ability to focus, and he sat in his chair gaping.

That shock and his reaction, though, transformed into blind rage.

He'd seen Rafe walking with his niece. She'd recently made drastic changes in her life, coming out of her extended mourning. Dressing like the lass, nay, the woman, she was.

Only one thing helps a person do that. The affection of another.

Robert stood again, and this time, lifted his chair and threw it against the wall where it burst into a fall of wooden shards.

Duncan and Nevan didn't flinch. They remained as angered and focused on Robert.

"How do ye know for certain?" he growled.

Nevan told Robert of their encounter with the MacKays.

"Ye killed them all?"

Nevan nodded. "I believe we did."

"And Rafe, he rained blows upon his own men?"

"Whether to assist us or to hide his lies, I dinna ken, but aye."

Robert rubbed his hand over his face.

"The MacKays shall retaliate, undoubtedly. We'll prepare for that after we handle this Rafe character. Where is the man now?" Robert asked through gritted teeth.

"We dumped him into the empty croft, bound. He awaits your decision."

Robert clenched his jaw, considering. His role as leader had grown in the past year, and now he faced a decision that he never expected he'd have to make — this was Kevin's job.

But after the recent conversations he'd had with Anne, how Kevin didn't recognize his daughter at all, how he thought Robert still a lad and Maud still alive, the leadership issue within the Fraser clan had come to a head. 'Twas time to act. They'd let the subject of the Laird's diminished faculties linger for too long. Anne had assured him that everyone in the clan was ready to back Robert's assumption of the Lairdship; the only thing he had to do was step into the role.

The moment was now. And Robert stepped.

"Duncan, Nevan. We have a few concerns that must be dealt with. First, the Laird's health has taken a turn for the worse, and he will never recover. We must have a new Laird."

"Ye, o'course," Duncan interjected. "All the men will support ye. Dinna doubt it. Ye had stood in the Laird's stead for a long time. Ye should be the Laird in truth now."

Robert flicked his eyes to Nevan, who nodded his approval.

"I'll draw up the agreement, if ye, Duncan, will have the men sign it. Since there is no son of age . . . "

"I'll see to it, Laird," Duncan responded.

Robert pursed his lips at the title but tipped his head and accepted it. He'd known it was coming, he just didn't anticipate it under such dire conditions.

"Now, we have this man who ye say is a MacKay. Though we've been victims of some of the worst those vile MacKays had to offer, we dinna ken the man's position against us years ago. He may be no more than an innocent in that clan. Until we can discern that —"

"What of his transgressions against us?" Nevan interrupted. "His lying? His deceptions? And what of his association with our Brenna?"

The hard set in Robert's jaw returned at the mention of his niece.

"That we must determine as well. I tasked ye with watching her. Especially when she dresses as her brother, she trespasses where she oft should not."

Duncan and Nevan had the good sense to look contrite and drop their faces to the floor.

"When we are home, our guard is down. We expected her to be safe among her own," Robert added.

"But she wasn't with her own, was she? She was with that MacKay," Duncan said with spite.

A tense silence fell among the men, then Robert waved it away.

"It does no' matter. I, too, failed in keeping her guarded from him. We welcomed him. We're all at fault here."

"Ye dinna think he overstepped?"

Robert swallowed hard, trying not to choke on the thought of that black bear of a MacKay lying with his vulnerable niece.

"I dinna want to think on it. Let's find out what he has to say for himself."

"Should we find Brenna? Ask her what she knows? She's spent time conversing with him."

A knock at the door frame drew the men's attention. Duncan and Nevan were blocking the door and glanced over their shoulders to see the fair Dawn behind them, a fretful expression shadowing her normally bright face.

"I dinna mean to intrude, but I heard ye from the hallway."

Robert wiggled his fingers to invite her into the constricted space of the study.

"What concerns ye, lass?" Robert asked.

His mind reeled. *What now?* He tried to keep his tone level, though he was irritated that Dawn was here when they needed to confront the MacKay.

She cleared her throat and withdrew a small item from her skirts. 'Twas a dirk, and she set it on the desk near Robert. He lifted it, suddenly more interested in the reason for Dawn's presence.

"What do ye have here?"

"Dorcas found it with that Rafe's belongings, under his pallet. 'Tis a MacKay dirk, aye?" She looked to Robert for confirmation. He barely glanced at it.

"Aye, 'tis a MacKay dirk."

Dawn squinted at the man. He didn't appear surprised at her question.

"Ye know already."

She had always been a quick study and able to read people well. Robert's expression revealed nothing.

"How long have ye had this?" he asked instead.

"Since this afternoon."

"Ye are only bringing it to me now?"

"I brought it to Brenna first," Dawn admitted.

Robert's terse face lifted and caught Duncan's gaze. So, Brenna did know.

"What did she say?"

"I told her we dinna ken if he found it, stole it, or if he is a MacKay. Brenna, I fear, assumes the worst."

"As well she should," Duncan commented from the doorway.

"Should we ask her about Rafe?" Nevan broached the topic that no one wanted to address. How deep did her affections for Rafe run?

"Dawn," Robert struggled to hold his voice in check, "what exactly is Brenna's relationship with this man?"

Dawn lifted her chin. 'Twould be easy for Dawn to assume — the lass's attentions on Rafe were undeniable. But had she taken it too far? That only Brenna could say. And seeing the severe lines of Robert's face, Dawn doubted Brenna would tell her uncle anything.

"I canna say for certain. But I believe she has feelings for the man. Deep feelings. Look at the changes she's made in recent weeks. He's the only thing that's new in her life that encouraged her to put the past behind her."

As much as Robert hated to hear the truth, 'twas obvious when he considered Dawn's words.

"Christ's blood." He rubbed his hand across his beard as he weighed his options. "We must confront this Rafe first. Find out his true identity and hear from his lips what's trespassed with Brenna. Then we can speak to my niece."

Duncan didn't need to be told twice. He spun and stormed down the hall, followed closely by Nevan and Robert.

***

They slammed the worn wooden door when they left, shaking a layer of thatch dirt onto Rafe's head.

He took a moment to wallow in self-pity, watching the dust settle in the darkness. The sun had set on this conflicting day, and Rafe's head was swimming at all that had transpired.

He should feel troubled. He should be worried about his future. But the only thoughts in his head were of Brenna, of her delicate skin atop his plaid, of losing his hands in her rich tresses, of her words of love.

All of which Rafe was about to lose. His lie, though told for noble intentions, could well send her back into hiding. And he didn't want to face her. Rafe couldn't bear to see the repercussions his lie had wrought.

Banging his fists in frustration against the ground dirtied his hands and wiggled the ropes where they bound him to the wall. His brow furrowed with curiosity. Rafe banged the ground again, his arm muscles flexing against his tunic, and the post snapped, allowing him to slip the ropes off his wrists.

The Frasers must have been preoccupied to have not secured him well.

Moving quickly to unravel his arms and hands, Rafe dropped the rope and crawled to the door where a jagged hole gave him a decent view of the rear of the keep.

He saw no guard, no Frasers. That didn't mean they weren't there. Holding his breath that his luck held out, he stood and threw his weight against the door which burst open in protest.

No Fraser came at him.

Fortune, finally, was on his side.

With a dejected glance back at the tower and thoughts of Brenna searing his mind, Rafe broke into a run, racing for the woods as his plaid flapped against his thighs.

In the dark, the only visible part of him was his eyes reflecting moonlight. He slipped into the woods and disappeared into the brush.

He did what he should have done days before. He finally left the Frasers.

Rafe noted he needed to head south, find his way to the Bruce, but the Fraser lands blocked him. And 'twas what they would expect him to do. He decided to work his way northwest, then south on the far side of the loch. In the thick of night, that was a harrowing journey. While getting far from the Fraser clan was of immediate import, he then could camp under the stars and resume his travels in the morn.

Once he felt he was far enough to take a break, Rafe camped for the night. Wrapped in his *breacan* at the base of a tree, he slept fitfully, his haggard sleep plagued with nightmares of Brenna when she learned the truth about him. The morning was still draped in darkness when he stopped fighting the dreams and stared at the black, leafy canopy above him.

A rustling noise caught his attention, and his skin pricked. Was another boar hiding in the brush? Rafe rolled over and listened. 'Twas far too early for boars — they weren't crepuscular animals. What was that sound?

He followed his ears, stepping as lightly as the underbrush would allow, until he came upon a gathering of men snoring around a campfire, each cocooned in their own plaid. From behind an old, thick tree, Rafe watched as one man returned to the sleepers, probably having relieved himself, and curled up for another hour or so of sleep.

MacKay men. A lot of them. Rafe recognized the men and their plaids. Somehow they learned that their raiding party had failed and paid for that failure with their lives. Had one of the men escaped?

Squinting in the moonlight, Rafe studied the men. Each was equipped with a broadsword at the ready, and if Rafe knew his men, several dirks of all sizes were also tucked in their braies, kilts, and boots.

They were not coming to raid more cattle. The number of heavily armed men resting only a few miles north of the Fraser land told him enough. They were ready for a battle.

And the Frasers were focused on a lone man they believed they had bound in a croft. They were not prepared for this.

Rafe snuck back to where he had stopped for the night, right off the worn trail leading through the grove of trees. His eyes flicked south, to where the Bruce somewhere resided. 'Twas the path of least resistance. Rafe could continue on his way this morn, arrive in the Lowlands within days, and join up with the Bruce.

And never see Brenna again.

And worse — leave her to the machinations of the MacKays.

If anyone knew the danger the MacKays may wreak on an unprepared clan, 'twas Rafe.

He looked to the east.

To the Fraser lands.

To Brenna.

They would kill him as soon as he entered the keep. He'd be fortunate if they didn't torture him first.

Yet his heart made the decision before his brain.

Flipping his *breacan* over his shoulders, Rafe made his way back to the trail and started toward the Fraser lands. With a final glance in the direction of the MacKay camp, he broke into a run.

The gray line of sunrise stretched across the horizon, and Rafe raced on to make it to Broch Invershin before the MacKays woke.

Chapter Fifteen: Vengeance

The horses exploded from the trees, directly at Rafe. Robert and Duncan yanked back on the reins and Robert's steed reared up, its dangerous hooves dancing in the air above Rafe's head before crashing to the earth near his feet.

Once Rafe caught his breath, he raised his eyes to the angry visages of the Fraser men growling in front of him.

In matching movements, Robert and Duncan leapt from their horses to Rafe, grabbing at him. Robert's face was inches from Rafe's, his fury emanating from his skin like a fire.

"Ye abuse our hospitality, take liberties with my niece, and we find ye are no' who ye say? Instead, ye are my worst enemy? And what will happen to ye is naught compared to what I will do if I learn ye have been inappropriate with Brenna. Ye will pray for death."

"Robert, I must speak with ye!" Rafe implored.

"Unless ye are confessing and throwing yourself on my mercy, I dinna want to hear from ye."

"Nay, Robert, I beg —"

Rafe was not prepared for the hit from the hulking Duncan that snapped his jaw as sharp as a hammer. Rafe collapsed to his knees, with only the fierce grip of Robert and Duncan holding his arms keeping his upper body upright.

Trying to regain his senses, Rafe moved his jaw, testing it to see if 'twere broken. He managed to move it with only the resonating pain of the punch. He had to try again, force Robert to hear him.

Before he could speak, they had bound his hands behind him and threw him over the rear haunches of Duncan's horse. He spent the short ride back to Broch Invershin jouncing until he thought he'd lose his stomach. He tried shouting to make himself heard, but his voice was lost in the wind and galloping of the horses.

They reached the bailey, and Duncan hauled him off the horse and dumped him on the ground. Rafe was not a small man by any means, and this manner of strength sent a shiver of trepidation across his wame.

Rafe could handle battle; he could well hold his own in a fight, but against a mountain of a man like Duncan, or Duncan and his men all at once? Rafe would put up a good fight, but 'twould not end in Rafe's favor, that he well knew.

Rafe struggled to regain his feet, and Duncan shoved him back to the dirt. Dust filled his mouth, and he spat before trying to speak again.

"Robert, please. Ye dinna ken what's in the trees!"

Robert stood over him, a plaid-clad figure in the long shadows of sunrise. The day was growing brighter, and Rafe knew that the MacKays were going to strike before full light. 'Twas their way.

"I dinna want to hear ye —"

"Ye will!" Rafe roared, his voice echoing in the yard. "The MacKays are on their way!"

Robert couldn't stop the punch which fell as Rafe spoke, but pulled it, so his fist only glanced off the side of Rafe's face. 'Twould leave a bruise, but Rafe shook it off.

"The MacKays?"

"In retribution for the attack yesterday. They have marched through the night and rested just north of here. They will be here soon — any moment! To strike before dawn is their way!"

Rafe prayed they listened to him. He had no motive to lie.

Robert and Duncan shared a dire look. A sneak attack? They'd had minor skirmishes with the MacKays since Braden and Maud's deaths, reived cattle and sheep, but nothing like a full charge on Fraser land since that dark time. Duncan spun at his men.

"Nevan! Kellan! Wake the men! To arms!"

Robert grabbed at Duncan's *breacan*. "We must split up the men. 'Twill weaken us, but we dinna ken where they will attack first. They canna have many, but the clans are short on men who are with the Bruce."

Rafe sat in the dirt and noted the intensity in the Fraser men's eyes. Their bodies were tight, ready for combat, and several had already pulled their swords, claymores calling for blood. Rafe had a flash of inspiration.

"Robert, please. Listen to me once more."

The new Laird twisted in anger, clutching Rafe's tunic in a fierce grip. "What more do ye have to say, ye lying traitor?"

"Nay! Please. Ye dinna have to split up your men. Release my hands. I will approach the MacKays under the guise of having spied on ye and direct them where ye want. Do ye have a place where they might funnel, where your men might have the upper hand?"

The sun fought against them, the beacon of light broadening on the horizon. They had to work fast. Robert, though, didn't speak right away. Instead, with twitching amber eyes he studied the MacKay man on the ground in front of him, weighing the man's words.

If he trusted Rafe, it could well lead the Frasers to victory, give them a measure of vengeance against the MacKays, and defeat them finally.

If Rafe were lying, the MacKays could lay waste to the Frasers, men, women, land. Was it worth the risk?

He had no choice. Robert slipped his dirk into his hand and swiped it betwcen Rafe's hands in one swift move, cutting his bindings. He threw Rafe's sword at him where it clanged in the dirt.

"Get up. The stones there," Rafe told him, pointing to a set of trees and boulders near the gate, "if ye tell them that it leads to the back of the keep where they might sneak up on us, they may believe ye and have to narrow to come through. Then my men can attack."

Rubbing his wrists, Rafe grabbed his broadsword and ran off, back down the trail leading past the gate. Duncan gave a loud yell at this development.

"Ooch! Robert! Have ye lost all your senses?"

The new laird despised the words, thinking them too close to his brother's condition. He glowered at Duncan, then shoved him toward his men.

"Gather your men. Half in the brush leading to the stones by the gate. The rest inside the gate, near the rear of the keep. Rafe is going to mislead the MacKays and give us a chance to defeat them."

***

Dawn was in Brenna's room, brushing out the gown that Brenna had unceremoniously cast to the side in her sorrow. Instead, Brenna had pulled on a pair of braies and one of Braden's oldest, softest tunics and curled up into a ball on the bed. Dawn had been correct — Brenna had cared for the dark stranger with such ferocity, and now her fragile heart was breaking into pieces once again. Moving to the bed, Dawn smoothed Brenna's lustrous locks from her forehead, a motherly touch that the wee, confused lass needed.

Brenna's brow was damp, fevered, and Dawn reached to the window slit to pull the tapestry aside. A flash of color caught her attention. She bumped Brenna's table as she moved to get a better look, and Brenna awoke.

"Dawn? What are ye doing?" Brenna asked in a hoarse voice, scratchy from a night of sobbing.

Dawn didn't answer, her eyes riveted on the sight of Rafe running down the path and followed by several Fraser warriors slipping silently into the woods.

"Dawn?" Brenna rose, joining her at the window. Her eyes followed the direction of Dawn's gaze.

Leaning her face out, she saw what Dawn had — the back end of Rafe racing away amid the scattering of Fraser men.

"Dawn!" she exclaimed, stepping back to her bed. "What's going on?"

"I dinna ken," Dawn answered. She rested her hand at her neck in a nervous gesture. "Let's go to the kitchens and see what is amiss."

"Why was Rafe running away? Is he escaping?" Brenna queried as they made their way down the narrow stone steps toward the kitchens. Dawn glanced over her shoulder.

"Brenna, I dinna ken," she repeated. "But if he were escaping, why were the Frasers letting him run?"

They reached the kitchen where Dorcas and Sarah were already busy preparing oat cakes and parritch. Their strained faces meant they had heard or seen something that distressed them.

"What's amiss?" Dawn asked.

Sarah's pale lips remained tight, but Dorcas leaned toward Dawn.

"I heard something regarding the MacKays. I did no' hear what exactly."

"Do ye ken where the men are going?" Dawn flicked her eyes to Brenna and back. "Or Rafe?"

"Naught but shouting."

Dorcas words served as a harbinger, for a raucous uproar rang from the rear of the keep — just outside the kitchen doors. A flurry of Fraser warriors swarmed the keep and surrounded the yard.

Dawn scrambled to the kitchen door and slammed the iron bar into place, barring them against the pandemonium on the other side.

High, narrow window slits were the only opening to the yard. Dorcas tried to peer into the main hall, only to be countered by Kellan standing guard over the keep's interior with two other young Fraser men. He took up the entire space of the archway to the hall, fearsome and immense.

"Ye women are to remain here. Ye barred the door?" he asked, looking over at the thick door that separated them from the fracas. Shouts and the clanging of swords made the women jump.

Dorcas nodded, mute with fear. Kellan's eyes searched the room.

"The door is solid, and the laird's men are safeguarding it. These men and myself are at the main door to the hall, holding that entry. There should be no breach, but if there is, ye make for the cellars, ye ken?"

All four women paled at his words and cuddled together in silent support. Brenna had been young when her brother died and didn't recall much of earlier encroachments by the MacKays. Recent interactions had been little more than reiving a cow here or there. But this . . .

This manner of attack, 'twas familiar to Dorcas and Dawn. Even Sarah recalled a few of the MacKays' more violent assaults. They'd thought this panicked waiting was over, that after the MacKays ruined the heart of the Frasers, they would stay away.

The presence of the MacKays on Fraser land, a large enough number to bring every Fraser warrior to his feet with sword in hand, meant Dorcas and Dawn were wrong.

The women in the kitchens had unconsciously formed a loose circle around Brenna, as though they could protect her from the horrors of the world. Kellan was glad to see it. Brenna was the last of Laird Kevin's family. While the man might no longer be Laird, his brother had no children sprung from his own loins. Brenna was the last of their line.

If she didn't realize it, everyone else in the clan did. She wasn't guarded solely because of her strange dressing proclivities or desires to act like a lad; she was protected because she was the only one who remained. Kevin's illness may have ended his laird ship, yet that didn't mean it ended anyone's loyalty to him, to Robert, or to Brenna.

Frasers were loyal to a fault. They would guard Brenna with their lives.

***

Rafe raced up the road with nothing more than his broadsword strapped to his back and his wits against the MacKays. He needed to persuade whoever led the MacKays to attack to the rear in a large group. To convince them that he was spying for their side was paramount.

At first, he feared his ability, but then he realized he'd spent the past months living a lie. If anything, he had mastered the art of deception. Surely, he could beguile the wayward MacKays.

An older man Rafe didn't recognize at once commanded the troupe toward the Fraser land. His plaid was dirty and ragged, as was his light brown and gray beard. Rafe emerged from the brush, a finger to his lips.

"They dinna ken we approach. I have seen the best way in," Rafe said with conviction.

"Rafe! I did no' ken ye were with us!"

Cursing under his breath, Rafe gave the leader a tight smile. Rafe's brain recalled the man in a sudden rush. *Ren. His name is Ren.*

"Aye, Ren. I left a while ago, studying the clans nearby. Better to try for a herd than one or two cows, aye? The Frasers, they have been the most lax in their guard."

Ren raised a curious eyebrow. "Unlike yesterday?"

He was referring to the slaughter the Frasers had imparted on the small band of thieving MacKays from the day before — the men who had recognized him.

"I think 'twas due to the number of cattle taken. And that was the first time I'd seen the clan act. To avoid that again, I ken a way to breach the land, the keep even, if ye want food, wine, and women."

The grumblings of the men riding behind Ren became hoots and huzzahs at the prospect of liquid and parted legs. Rafe kept his own face loose, even as every part of him tensed, wanting to slay these men for their dishonorable intentions.

"What is your strategy?" Ren asked, waving a hand at the randy men to calm them.

"As ye approach the gate, dismount. No sounds of the horses. Then round the stones to the rear. It leads to the back of the keep, where there's naught but a weak, unguarded kitchen door. Breach that, and ye have access to the keep."

The men brightened at the possibility of an easy conquest as Ren studied Rafe, judging his words. Rafe held his breath, keeping his face bland. This was the moment. Ren might cut him down with a swift swing of his claymore or believe him and lead the men unknowingly to disaster.

Several heartbeats passed before Ren turned his gaze to the path.

"The stones?"

"Aye, east of the postern gate. Go silently, on the edges of the road, and the keep and the Fraser land will be yours."

Ren nodded at Rafe in thanks, then circled his arm over his head for the men to follow him. Rafe fell in with the crowd of more than thirty scraggly men. Not large enough for a full attack, so they were definitely looking for an ambush, wanting to deal another quick, harsh blow to the Frasers.

And Rafe's encouragement to attack from the rear fit their plans perfectly. Just as Rafe knew it would. Banal predictability was a weakness.

As Rafe walked alongside the riders, he had a flash.

Predictability.

From her dressing as a lad, to her uncommon kin, to how her clan shielded their laird's family, Brenna and the Frasers were anything but predictable. Every time he thought he might have Brenna figured out, she did something, made a comment, that caught him off guard.

That's what attracted him to her at the outset. That's why he kept searching her out and was open to her affections.

It's why, he was forced to admit, that he loved her. All of her mad, broken ways, they only endeared her to him. And the only thing he wished to do was hold her, hug her until every broken piece came back together.

From what he'd seen, Rafe had been doing a decent job of that already. He didn't know when it happened, but ever since he watched her rise from the loch like a nymph from folklore, his life had changed. *He* had changed. Brenna had changed. If she found someone to love, someone who loved her back in that strange, crazed love, who knows what else she might show him? What other layers he might find? What other passions might he uncover?

Rafe kept his sights straight ahead as his mind whirled in a frenzy. He wanted to run back to Broch Invershin, sweep Brenna up in his arms, and declare his love as he found her lips. Claim her for his own in front of her entire clan. It took every ounce of will not to show this epiphany of love to his old clan. Instead, he had to continue to march at a clipped pace, right next to the very men who would find their demise at the tip of his sword.

Because he couldn't let the men who had wounded Brenna so deeply live. Rafe didn't know which of these men had a hand in the death of Brenna's brother. Ren, presumably. Rafe knew him to be a fierce warrior and one who prided himself on subduing the nearby clans. 'Twas no doubt in Rafe's mind that Ren, if he hadn't led the attack against the Frasers years ago, was involved in the battle, nonetheless.

Rafe let his fiery gaze fall on the man. *Ye shall be first,* Rafe vowed.

Ren's death would be the first in Rafe's vengeance on behalf of Brenna and her family. The MacKays would see the warrior they had wrought, and the Frasers could then meet the man who'd given up everything for the woman he loved.

Rafe's eyes scanned the woods as they closed in on the stones. Swatches of plaid blended in with the trees, camouflaged in the brush. The Fraser men were lying in wait, anticipating the moment when the MacKays were most vulnerable. 'Twas a reversal of history.

Then they were threading the needle between the stones, and the cacophony of the Fraser Highland charge reverberated across the land. Ren's face hardened as he drew his broadsword against the onslaught of men, and he glared back at Rafe before his own battle cry joined the chaos.

Rafe wasted no time. Ren understood Rafe's subterfuge, and his moment was now. Ren would come for him if he had the chance, and Rafe needed to bring the man low before Ren's sword found his back.

Three steps brought Rafe directly beside Ren's horse, where Ren's thighs clenched the saddle as he swung his broadsword around, metal clanging on metal against a Fraser — Kellan. Ren was occupied, and Rafe's steps launched him at Ren's backside, knocking the older man from his steed just as his own sword slipped against the yielding skin of the man's side. Blood slicked Rafe's blade, staining his hands, his plaid, and the ground under them.

Ren was quick — faster than Rafe had estimated. Though injured, 'twasn't a mortal wound and the man rolled to his feet, his free hand pressing against the gash at his waist. Fury poured from Ren like the blood from his wound.

"Ye were always a coward, Rafe. Attacking me from behind."

"Really, ye say this as ye are attacking the Frasers from the rear? What manner of warrior are ye? None." Rafe spit at the man's feet to punctuate his insult.

"Ye talk of warriors? Ye are nothing. A man who betrayed his clan!" Ren's voice was strong, even when he was injured. He held his sword in a strong hand.

"I am a warrior who came to the aid of a clan in need. 'Tis more than ye can claim."

"Ha!" Ren spouted a mocking laugh. "And who are ye? I canna believe that ye told these Frasers who ye are. No' if ye wanted to live."

"They know now. And here I am, fighting ye, no' them. I think that tells all."

Rafe was done talking. He lunged forward at a clip. Ren countered and spun, but the slit at his side was significant, bleeding more than he realized, and his movement was slow. His sword only caught the edge of Rafe's tunic, ripping it. Then, when Ren raised his sword to bring it down against Rafe, his thrust was weak and missed its mark.

Taking advantage of Ren's weakened state, Rafe feinted and thrust against Ren, this time catching Ren's other side, his blade hitting the mark as it slid deep beneath the man's skin.

Ren froze on Rafe's sword, then his body went limp. Rafe thrust the blade harder, digging in and twisting. When Ren fell, Rafe wanted to ensure the man would not rise again.

Ren's sword clanged to the ground seconds before Ren landed, falling in a solid heap and a pool of blood that stained the earth a wet black. The sun peeked above the horizon, its pale light illuminating Ren's death pallor.

He would victimize the Highland clans no more.

Certain Ren was down, Rafe spun on his toes and entered the fray with the rest of the Frasers. The giants of Broch Invershin had risen to the occasion, laying waste to the MacKays who were unprepared for the surprise turnabout assault. 'Twas a blitz, swift and stringent, and the Fraser men stood amid the bodies and death, blood dripping from sword tips and chests panting in exertion.

This time, unlike years ago, the surprise attack favored the Frasers, who lost no men. This time they reigned victorious against the MacKays who'd wreaked such havoc over the past years.

At least for the Frasers, the MacKays' reign of terror had come to an end.

Their years of anguish were over.

Chapter Sixteen: What the Heart Wants

They would send the remains of the fallen back to the MacKay clan, giving them a day to claim their dead before the Frasers disposed of them in a funeral pyre. The priest might protest for a Christian burial, but that final decision fell on Robert.

Meanwhile, the men, Rafe included, made their way back to the front of the keep where an audience of Fraser women and children cheered their men and rushed to embrace them — to know they were real and alive and had returned.

'Twas not missed by anyone that Anne, who had joined Brenna, Dawn, and Dorcas in the kitchens when she retrieved Kevin's morning meal, strode from the stairs to Robert, kissing him in full view of the clansmen and women. Like Rafe, she no longer hid her affections for the burly new Laird. They had denied their love out of respect for their positions caring for Kevin and his clan, but with the changes as of late, this one was an easy choice to make.

Rafe searched the landing for Brenna, thinking she must have been standing near Anne, when a rough hand yanked at the back of his neck. Rafe twisted against the hand, trying to get a look at his captor.

"Dinna fight me, MacKay," Duncan commanded. Rafe's own name sounded strange when said aloud.

"Wait, what are ye doing?"

"I'm taking ye to our Laird, so we can decide what must be done with ye."

"Done with me?" Rafe struggled to free himself. Duncan had to be mistaken. Had he not seen and heard what Rafe had done for the Frasers? "But I —"

Rafe managed to get his hand up, clamping it over Duncan's hand as he spun around. Duncan shifted his grip, going for Rafe's throat and grabbed at his arms, trying to immobilize Rafe. They scuffled, and Duncan swept a foot behind Rafe's leg, and he spilled to the ground in a heavy thud. Duncan was on top of him in a flash, working to bind Rafe's hands.

Rafe was perplexed. While he'd hidden his true identity and lied to the Frasers, he'd done it for a good reason, and when the moment mattered, he fought for the Frasers against his own clan. He'd proven his loyalty to the clan! Why was he now bound and being dragged to a prison cell again?

Duncan didn't take him to a cell. Their fight had garnered the attention of those in the yard, and furious glares greeted him as Duncan dragged him in the dirt to Robert. Lady Anne had stepped away, giving Robert the space he required to contend with the treacherous Rafe.

Throwing Rafe near Robert's feet, Duncan joined the Fraser men who had formed a loose circle around their Laird. Rafe was now at the center of attention he didn't want, that he didn't deserve. Rafe prayed that Brenna was yet abed and wasn't present to bear witness to this low moment. He wanted to be her champion, her warrior, and instead he was bound, writhing in the dust in a filthy, ripped tunic, a prisoner of the Frasers. Shame and bewilderment consumed him.

Rafe's hands were knotted together with a leather thong in front of him, and he stood before Robert, his palms up, placating.

"Robert, what is this?"

Robert's severe gazed sized up the man before him. His face showed nothing, but Robert was conflicted. The man standing before him had fought for the Frasers, gave them a strategy for success, and wore MacKay blood on his torn tunic and sword. Rafe should be celebrated for his actions.

But this same man had lied to the Frasers for weeks, hidden his true identity about a clan Robert despised with every ounce of his soul, and mayhap seduced his fragile niece. That last thought caused him to grimace. The lass had intentionally veiled herself away to avoid this very breach!

Rafe may have contributed to the Fraser victory, but the man was still a scoundrel. Robert could not tolerate a scoundrel.

One did not permit the fox to live in the hen house.

***

With a sudden shift of his body, Robert lunged at Rafe, his hammer fist catching Rafe's chin, and an explosion of pain rocking his face. The hit knocked him back. If his hands and been bound behind him, Rafe would have fallen arse over ankles. As it was, he managed to keep his feet, shaking off the punch. He was unsteady on his feet, as though the Laird had given his brains a stir with the strike to go with the bruised jaw.

Robert inhaled, pulling himself up to his full height, scant inches shorter than the MacKay warrior. Every ounce of anger had gone into that strike, yet Robert still burned. Brenna — she was the reason the fury smoldered beneath his skin. Robert forced himself to believe that his niece had not been alone with Rafe, that the craven man hadn't stolen even a precious drop of her innocence. She'd survived so much, the idea that this degenerate MacKay touched her, stole a meager kiss, might break her in a way unimaginable.

He could barely handle her mannerisms as it was. Robert didn't know if he had the fortitude to care for her if she escaped deeper into her fantasy world. Or worse, thinking she'd never overcome this transgression and took her own life. Echoes of Maud reverberated in his mind, and Robert shuddered. The clan, his brother, even Robert himself, would never recover from such a harrowing event.

Standing over the crouched MacKay, who cringed as he rubbed at his injured jaw, Robert waited to see what Rafe said on his behalf.

"Ye have abused our hospitality, MacKay. We opened our clan to ye, our home to ye, and this is what ye do? Lie to us? Hide your affiliation with our worst enemy? Trespass with my beloved niece?"

All sound in the yard immediately halted at those final words. Duncan, Nevan, and Kellan had the good sense to lower their eyes, acknowledging their lax guard of Brenna, believing it to be a banal chore. The accusation hung heavy in the bailey while Robert studied Rafe's reaction.

The man's blue eyes blazed at the indictment — but not as a reaction of innocence. A blaze of resentment, of a man whose lover is insulted before he throttles the offender.

That was the moment Robert knew. His niece had eluded her guards, had been alone with this lecher, and had her innocence possibly compromised. Robert's lips pulled into a hard grimace.

"Did ye think she'd want ye, man?" Robert mocked Rafe in a guttural voice. "Ye couldn't have kept your identity a secret forever. Did ye think she'd be with ye once she knew who ye are?"

Robert leaned in to Rafe, his rough beard scratching against Rafe's own skin. "No one wants ye, the degenerate that ye are. Ye are no' worthy of living."

***

Rafe scrambled back, shock at this turn of events making it difficult to think clearly. He'd just helped this clan defeat an old enemy. He'd helped Brenna come out of her shell. Hell, he'd even saved her life in the wood! And this Fraser man claimed he wasn't worthy?

He managed to put several paces between the two of them, but that didn't halt Robert, who raged with blood lust that had been incited with the vicious battle against the MacKays. He was worked up, and now Rafe was in his sights.

Rafe's frantic eyes searched the yard, trying to find an out, an escape, a way to cool Robert's heated enmity.

Nothing. No Fraser man came forward. The Fraser women stood behind the wall of men, some with eyes just as angry as Robert's, other cowering at the events unfolding before them.

As Rafe's gaze swung back to Robert, the bulky laird took a menacing step toward him, reaching above his head to draw his claymore from the scabbard on his back. The ring of the blade sent a chill over those gathered in the bailey.

Rafe froze. This man had just slaughtered several MacKays. Surely, his blood lust was sated. Why draw his sword?

The dreadful expression cast a shadow across Robert's face, a sense of purpose — and that purpose as to strike Rafe down.

***

Though his wrists were bound, Rafe extended his hands as best he could over his shoulder, trying to grab at the pommel of his broadsword still strapped to his back. His torn tunic hindered him almost as much as his bindings. The odds were horribly stacked against his survival, but at his core, Rafe was a warrior. He'd not let Robert kill him without a fight.

Before Robert pressed forward, a high-pitched screech made them twist around, turning their attention to a flash of brown rushing down the steps.

Brenna, dressed in her brother's clothes, launched herself in front of Rafe's exposed, panting chest, shielding him with her body. The willful lass glared at her uncle, their eyes mirroring matching flames of indignation and fury.

"Bren, dinna involve yourself," Robert cautioned. "I dinna ken what he's done to ye, but he must pay for his transgressions. All of them."

Brenna pursed her lips at her uncle's implication.

"Nay, Uncle. This man has done nothing that I did not permit."

Rafe groaned behind her. 'Twas not a ringing endorsement of her innocence, which the crowd in the yard now presumed correctly that she no longer owned.

"Lass," Rafe whispered so low that only Brenna heard, "dinna get involved. Too much has happened here, and your uncle has the right of it. I can no' take advantage of ye and your hospitality anymore. 'Tis time for me to pay for my crimes."

Brenna flapped her hand at Rafe to silence him.

"Sheathe your sword, Uncle. Rafe's blood will no' spill this day."

"Brenna! Leave now," Robert commanded.

Brenna's response was to raise her chin in defiance.

"Nay. Enough blood has been sown with the MacKays. We've had our retribution against the clan that has taken so much. But we are better than they are. I am better than they are. My brother, my mother, even my father, they would no' want this! 'Tis time to let the past rest and move forward."

She flicked her face over her shoulder at Rafe, giving him a reassuring smile before staring her speechless uncle down again.

"And as much as ye may no' care for it, my heart wants to move forward with Rafe. Perchance if our clans shared blood instead of shed blood, we might put this feud and all its terrible history behind us."

Pale with shock, Robert clutched his chest. His words came out in a breathless rush.

"Ye canna be serious. My niece, the daughter of my own blood, would take on a name so despised in our clan we dinna see fit to speak it? Your father will have my head if I let ye take on the name MacKay."

"I'm no' a MacKay," Rafe finally spoke. "I've no' been one for months. When I left my clan and came here, I abandoned everything my clan stood for, including the name that came with it. I took the MacLeod name out of necessity. 'Twas no thought behind it. I dinna have a name."

Rafe stepped forward, standing next to Brenna. His features softened as he gazed at her captivating face that stole his heart.

"I would be honored to become a Fraser."

The collective gasp went unnoticed by Brenna and Rafe, who saw only each other. Had Robert and the rest of the Frasers not stood glowering at them, Rafe would have risked a kiss in full view of those gathered.

"Nay," Robert responded, disbelieving. "Ye would no' take on the lass's name. 'Tis no' done."

"Mayhap that is true," Rafe answered, stepping in front of Brenna to face Robert. "But I am a man without a name, without a clan. Yet Brenna brought me home, invited me in, and your people welcomed me. Brenna showed me how life can be if 'tis lived without pride, without hate. She opened my heart and gave me a place in this world."

Rafe paused, letting the words sink in as he scanned the crowd. Then, with his bound hands, he grasped one of Brenna's in an awkward hold.

"Ye have no sons. Brenna's only brother has found his reward in heaven. 'Tis possible for the Laird Fraser's name to be passed along this way. I will gladly take on the name of the place, the woman, who gave me a home."

With that he pulled Brenna against him, lifting his bound hands to embrace her as best he could, and kissed her shaking lips. Brenna's arms slipped around Rafe's waist, pulling him closer.

Dejected, Robert shuddered, and his sword dangled by his side.

"Stop. Stop, Rafe. Dinna kiss my niece before me like that. No' unless ye are wed."

The words on Robert's tongue were a thick paste, but what other option did he have? To have his beloved niece, the daughter of his heart, be a wife to this man with ties to his gravest enemy? Or to have him leave his niece sullied and unwed? Wedding the man to his lass was the lesser of two evils, two horrible, unspeakable evils. And if the man were here, Robert could keep a better eye on him.

Kevin may never forgive him. 'Twas Robert's good fortune his brother's mind was already gone. He might have lost it completely with this development.

A hard wall of muscle pressed against Robert's arm.

"Are ye sure of this, Robert?" Duncan asked. He was flanked by Nevan and Kellan. They were contrite in realizing their lax guard of the lass may have well led to a series of events and were searching for absolution. A way to atone. "We can dispatch the man for ye right now. Save ye the trouble and take the weight from ye."

Brenna and Rafe both went white hearing the man's offer, and Rafe disentangled himself from Brenna to set her behind him. She may want to thrust her body in front of his as a shield, but he couldn't let her do that, not again. These men might come for him, and Rafe wouldn't risk her safety.

Robert caught the movement out of the corner of his eyes and placed his arm across Duncan's chest.

"Nay. Leave them. My niece had the right of it. As much as I hate to acknowledge it, she speaks the truth. Too much death, too much bloodshed, too much loss. I will no' have my niece lose this man too."

Robert replaced his sword in the scabbard and stepped to Rafe. He peered behind the MacKay warrior, catching Brenna's gaze, the one so like his own. His whole body sagged with emotion for the lass. She reminded him so much of Maud, his heart ached.

"If ye want this man, Brenna, I will no' say nay. I'll stand in your father's stead. He will be happy just to see ye happy." Robert's shoulders curved in exhaustion. "We've no' had much happiness in a long time. This man, Rafe. Does he make ye happy, Brenna?"

It seemed as though the entire yard held its breath. Brenna's apprehensive face fell upon those gathered around them, mesmerized by the scene. The hard lines of Duncan's features, the guarded looks of Kellan and Nevan. The concern on the faces of Dawn and Anne. The desperation in her uncle's face, and the dark, handsome gentleness in Rafe. He looked at Brenna as though the sun rose and set with her, and every time she caught that fierce blue gaze staring at her, Brenna's heart stopped.

Everything about Rafe made her happy. However, that was not the question she needed to answer. She had known that deep in her chest, deep in her soul. The question was, did she make Rafe happy? Could he be content to remain with her? With the Fraser clan?

As Rafe captured her gaze, his lips upturned to that sly smile of his, the same smile he gave her when he first met Brenna at the loch, when he told her that he understood why she hid, when he compared her to a butterfly, when he held her after their moment of loving.

That smile was her answer. It permeated her skin and touched her heart.

"Aye, uncle. He makes me happy."

Chapter Seventeen: The Endings We Deserve

As soon as the words left her lips, Rafe worked his arms around her again, lifting her into the air to plant a solid kiss on her inviting lips.

"Are ye certain? I have naught, lass. No clan, no prospect, hell, no' even a name. All I can offer is my body, my sword. And my heart."

Brenna's face lit with joy at his words. "Weel, I have a clan that I can share, prospects for ye, and a name ye can have. And as long as I have your body and your heart, I'm content. Just as long as ye care for my heart as well."

"And the sword?"

Her face scrunched up in a wry expression. "I can handle my own sword. Ye can keep yours."

"The better to be your warrior with," Rafe teased back. Then his face grew somber. "But ye are truly the warrior here, Brenna. Today ye have saved my life just as much as any man with a sword. Ye are braver than any here could imagine. 'Twould seem I have little to offer. Will ye have me, Brenna?"

"Brave? A warrior?" she snorted. "Ye have offered me more than I thought possible. Ye gave me back life, a life I'd hidden from for so long. Ye are my warrior, Rafe. I'll take ye as ye are, happily."

"So ye will wed me then?"

"Aye," she said in a breathless voice.

Who would have thought that her life could change to such a bright future after so dark a past? That her world might shift in a moment, but in such a joyous way?

"Even though I'm a MacKay?"

She tipped her head up at him, those rosy lips curling into a knowing smile. She tapped his dusty nose with her fingertip.

"Are ye now?"

A surprising burst of laughter rumbled up through Rafe's chest.

"I suppose nay. I have no' been a MacKay in quite a while."

"And if ye wed me, ye are willing to be a Fraser?" The incredulity in her voice was unmistakable.

"I'm willing to be anything if it means I can be with ye."

***

Robert left the yard in a huff. His whole body ached and his mind boiled at what he had to do next. There was an excellent chance Kevin was unaware of what was going on and didn't recognize his own daughter enough to care that she was going to marry — or who she was going to marry. Regardless, Robert was compelled to share this unwelcome news. He had to pray that Kevin's mind was so gone he wouldn't acknowledge the news at all.

Anne caught up with him before he made it to the stairwell.

"Robert, please wait."

She placed a cool hand on his back. Robert was distraught, and she sought to help him release that strain.

"I feel as though I have failed my brother," Robert confessed in a halting voice. "I've let his daughter get involved with a MacKay, right under my nose. She's too innocent, too fragile, and I allowed him to take advantage. Now I have to tell my brother of my failings."

Anne pressed herself against his broad, heaving back, wrapping her arms around his waist. Robert was a powerful man, having supported the clan and his brother for so, so long. He needed someone to hold him upright under that weight. No one could be strong all the time.

"No' failings, Rob. Ye know that. The heart wants what the heart wants. She could have well fallen in love with the man had she known he was a MacKay. And they seem cut from the same cloth.

The hiding, ye ken? And look how far she's come in so short a time. Perchance the man is a match for the lass."

She squeezed her arms, and Robert's tension eased as he relaxed into her.

"Ye are a sage one, Anne. I am fortunate in ye." Robert pivoted to wrap her in his own embrace. "Now I just need to convince Kevin of that."

"Me thinks Kevin will be receptive. If he's aware at all. And I know ye will be kind as ye tell him. Ye are naught if not kind."

Robert kissed her forehead, then threaded his arm with Anne's and escorted her up the stairs to Kevin's room.

Sarah sat by the hearth sewing as Kevin slurped at parritch that dripped down his chin. Robert gave Sarah a quick smile before turning to Kevin. His heart broke as it always did at the sight of his powerful older brother brought so low. At least he was still here, still alive. For that, Robert was grateful.

Kevin grinned widely as Robert perched on the edge of the bed. Anne set Sarah on her way, closing the door as the lassie departed.

"Robbie! 'Tis good to see ye! Has it been a while since I've seen ye? It seems like it has . . ." His voice drifted off and his eyes flitted around the room. He was trying to remember. Robert patted his hand.

"Dinna fret, brother. I've seen ye recently. No matter that. I have some good news for ye. Are ye up for hearing it?"

A long-gone light brightened Kevin's face. He clapped, childlike.

"News? Good news? 'Tis the best manner of news!"

"Aye, that 'tis, brother."

Robert paused, considering the best way to tell Kevin while trying to figure out if his brother would know of whom he spoke. Kevin had lost so many memories of Brenna as of late.

"'Tis about Brenna."

"Brenna," Kevin asked, his eyes flitting again. He didn't recall the name.

"Aye, your daughter? The wee bronzed lass who wears men's clothes? Who looks like she's lost in a tent when she wears them?"

Kevin's expression softened at the description of his daughter. He may not recall her name, but to Robert, it appeared he recalled the lass. Before Robert could continue, a voice from the door commanded their attention.

"I rather think the clothes fit well enough, Uncle," Brenna said in a light-hearted tone.

"Brenna," Robert breathed, then regarded the man next to her with less exuberance. His voice went flat. "And Rafe."

Rafe bowed his head to Robert. "Fraser."

"Are ye here to see your da?" Robert asked Brenna.

She and Rafe stepped into the chambers. Her eyes never left her father's diminished shape in the bed.

"Aye. I thought it prudent they meet and to tell him the news."

Grasping Rafe's hand in her own, she pulled him toward the bed, giving Rafe a look at the man behind the rumors.

He wasn't sure what he expected, but whatever it was, the man in the bed was not it.

The old Laird wasn't just old — he appeared decrepit. And while some measures had been taken to wash the man's hair and tunic, several new stains ruined the tunic and a bit of egg hung from his shaggy hair.

His eyes though, the rich shade of dense moss, were bright. Contrary to what others had said, the man's eyes looked sensible enough.

"Father," Brenna's voice carried to Kevin. He lifted his head at the sound, his gaze landing on the lass.

"Braden? Is that you?" Kevin raised his torso to greet them, and then an instant of wistfulness stole into his face. "Nay. Brenna! What are ye doing here? I have no' seen ye in so long! And why are ye dressed like your brother? Trying to trick me again, my bairn, eh?" The old Laird waggled a long finger at her.

Her father's response transformed Brenna. Her body, tight with nerves when they first entered the room, slackened, easing and flowing from her like water over rocks.

"Who is this with ye, lassie? I dinna recognize him, do I?" A flair of panic rose in Kevin's face as he flicked his eyes between Anne and Robert.

"Nay, brother. Ye dinna ken this man."

Rafe extended his hand to grasp the old Laird's arm. Kevin only looked at it, as though Rafe held a snake aloft. With a gentle movement, Brenna grasped her father's hand in her own, and then placed Rafe's atop them all.

"Father, this man desires to wed me. We are here for your blessing."

"What? Brenna? Surely ye are no' old enough to be wed! Ye are just a bairn!"

Kevin managed to sit up straighter. Brenna leaned forward to embrace her poor father. How sorrowful it must be to have such loose memories, to not be able to rely on one's mind. She patted his head and sat back.

"Nay, Father. Look at me. I am a woman full grown."

Kevin squinted as he regarded her, disbelieving.

"But ye are still wearing a laddie's clothes, just as ye did as a child." Confusion made his voice thick. Brenna dropped her head.

"Aye, Father. Today, I am in a tunic and braies. As of late, though, I've started wearing gowns again. Ye say I resemble mother in them. I've heeded the words of my uncle, and I've been working to come out of my shell."

"As ye should, lassie. Ye are too bright a star to hide in the dark. And now ye are to marry?"

Brenna nodded, a coy smile spreading across her round cheeks.

"Aye, Father. He is Rafe. He seeks my hand, and better yet, to become a Fraser."

Kevin cheered at her words. "So ye won't leave me? Ye'll still live here after ye wed? Your mother had to leave . . ." his voice drifted off in wistful sadness.

Whether he recalled Brenna in the future or not, regardless of where she lived, this moment of his distress that she might leave him made her heart soar.

"We shall stay here with ye, Da." Brenna choked on the words.

Kevin fell quiet, and Brenna thought they were done, that her father's mind had gone off the trail once more, when he spoke.

"Have ye a gown, yet? I'm sure we have your mother's gown, and ye'd look fine in it. I would love to see ye in Maud's gown."

Kevin started searching around the bed, as though Maud's gown was there with him. Brenna looked to her uncle and Anne. Her mother's gown? She hadn't seen it in her room. Had it been removed? She blinked back tears in wonder that her father thought of such a sentiment.

"We will find it for ye, lassie," Robert promised. "I'm sure it's just tucked away in her chambers, and we missed it when we cleaned."

"I canna wait to see ye in it," Kevin whispered, his limpid eyes watering. "Do we have parritch? Is it time to eat?"

The topic changed, and Anne retrieved the wooden bowl of parritch for him. Brenna patted his hand.

Her moment of having her husband-to-be meet her father was over.

***

The priest stood on the stairs before the church doors, his deep fern-green vestments glorious in the rare, bright afternoon sun.

Most of the Frasers gathered to witness the event — some out of love, others out of curiosity. 'Twas only a fortnight since they'd seen the Laird's daughter regularly wearing a tunic and braies. Now here she stood, wearing the same gown her mother had worn a generation ago, standing on these same steps, wedding Kevin on another sunny day.

The gown, fitted across the breast and through the sleeves, fell straight to her feet, the creamy flax contrasting the scarlet reds of her *arasaid* tartan draped from shoulder to hip. Against the tartan, her bronze hair took on a reddish tone, a crimson nimbus that swished around her shoulders.

Dorcas and Sarah had collected a poesy of white Highland heather, a shade lighter than her kirtle, tied with a strip of the Fraser plaid. In her wedding finery, Brenna was all things white and red. And she sparkled with joy. No stained tunics or torn braies this day.

The reason for that joy stood at the top of the steps with the priest, resplendent in his own costume. A freshly laundered, borrowed tunic and a Fraser kilt gifted from Robert helped Rafe appear the full Highland warrior that he was. The red and black tartan flattered his fierce dark looks and bright eyes that matched the sky. To Brenna, he was a vision.

Rafe's plaid, which fell from his hips in casual folds and then draped over his shoulder, was a perfect match to Brenna's. As her uncle walked her up the steps of the church and gave her hand to Rafe, the couple embodied the Fraser legacy.

And that legacy, especially this new chapter, was welcome by all. With their painful past behind them, and so many new opportunities before them, 'twas as if the Fraser clan was reborn.

Robert bowed to Rafe and the priest, then joined Anne, who had escorted Kevin from his chambers to watch the nuptials.

When he had first set his watery eyes on Brenna, they had widened, and his face seemed to break.

"Maud?" he had asked in a croaky voice. Anne leaned her mouth to his ear and whispered.

Brenna took her father's hand and placed it on her cheek.

"No' quite, Father. Can ye try again?"

"Oh, that voice. I know that voice. Is that my wee Brenna?"

He recognized her! Well, at least her voice. She blinked back the hot tears that threatened to fall. She wouldn't cry on her wedding day.

"Aye, Da. I'm glad ye came to my wedding."

"Ooch, lassie!" Kevin cried, moving his gaze over her gown. "Your mother's kirtle? Are ye certain ye are no' my Maud? The likeness. . ." his voice drifted off and the light behind his eyes faltered. "Are we at a festival? What are we celebrating?"

And in a flash, he was gone. But for a moment Brenna had her father back — he was present at her wedding, and she took that singular moment to heart.

"We are at Brenna's wedding, Kevin," Anne had told him in her ever-soothing voice, calming him.

Now she was standing in the church courtyard, before the man who was to become her husband. She glanced over at her father, leaning on Robert, with Anne on his other side. Kevin's eyes still remained on her, and if possible, her heart soared even more.

A light tug on her hand brought her attention back to Rafe and the priest. Father Fraser wore a serious expression, but Rafe's wild blue eyes were soft and inviting, though his hand shook a wee bit. A smile tugged at her cheeks. While he may have appeared steady in his stance, he was just as nervous as she. Rafe gave her a wide, wavering smile.

"Are ye ready?" he asked.

Brenna squeezed his hand and exhaled. "Aye. I'm ready."

The priest raised his hands, garnering the crowd's attention, and introduced the couple. Brenna slipped a silver circlet on Rafe's thick finger, catching it on his knuckle. Rafe flexed once it was on, as though testing the sensation of the metal against his skin, then grasped Brenna's hands and slid a slender ring with flecks of gold on her finger. Those familiar flecks . . .

Her astounded gaze flew to Rafe, whose smile floundered at her expression.

"Is this my mother's ring?"

Rafe blinked back hot tears at her reaction, and a flush stained his already reddened cheeks.

"Aye. Your Uncle Robert gifted it to me for our wedding. He said that he'd been saving it for ye all these years."

She studied the ring, plying the finery with her thumb. Her mother's gown, her mother's ring. Brenna was closer to her mother than she imagined she could be. Her mother may not have been in attendance at her wedding, but Brenna felt assured that somewhere in Heaven, Maud was indeed looking down upon them, hopefully giving her blessing.

"And your vows," the priest interrupted Brenna's musings. "Brenna Morgan Fraser, do ye take this man, Rafe, in ill and in health, to love, honor, and obey, until ye are dead?"

"Aye," she answered in a shaky whisper. Rafe nodded, ready for his words.

"Rafe MacKay, do ye—"

"Stop." Rafe held up a hand to halt the priest's vows.

The shocked look on the priest's face mirrored the faces of the crowd. Robert stiffened, ready to rush the stair, and Duncan reached his hand for the pommel of his broadsword. If the man sought an escape from wedding the sole Fraser legacy, he would have many to answer to first.

"Dinna call me MacKay."

Father Fraser paused, his perplexed eyebrows pulling together. "'Tis your name, is it no'?"

Rafe shook his head, but his eyes never left Brenna.

"I gave up that name, that clan, months ago. I have naught felt less a MacKay than I do in this moment. And I am no' MacLeod. But with Brenna, the warrior lass who stole my heart, I'd be honored to be a Fraser."

The priest's eyebrows were busy, rushing to his forehead in disbelief. The witnesses in the yard released their tense posturing, their own surprise painted on their faces.

"Ye want the lass's name? 'Tis no' done!" the priest cried out.

Rafe tipped his head in a nonchalant gesture. "'Tis done here. Today. When I came to this clan, I had a new opportunity, a new life. I will no' go back to that old life, even if it means giving up that name. 'Tis no' my clan. The Frasers, and Brenna, are my kin now."

This time, Brenna's tears did flow. So much for her vow not to cry on her wedding day. But her brilliant smile was unimpeded by the tears.

Father Fraser emitted an aggravated sigh.

"Weel, then. Rafe Fraser, do ye take this woman, Brenna, in ill and in health, to love, honor, and protect, until ye are dead?"

"Aye, I vow."

"Ye have a dirk?"

Rafe withdrew a knife from his belt, the same cursed knife that Dorcas found, and he put it to good use, giving it to the priest. The priest had a light touch, flinching the blade across Rafe's hand, then Brenna's, and he wrapped their hands in a long swath of Fraser tartan.

Then he gave the Highland prayer over their hands, the mixing of their blood sealing their wedding vows. And 'twas done — they were husband and wife.

"Ye may kiss your bride," the priest directed Rafe, who didn't hesitate.

He swept Brenna's lithe body off her feet in a passionate kiss that sent the crowd into a frenzy of cheers.

***

After the feast in celebration of their union (which Rafe noted had been stilted at times, but still astounding given the strange course of events), Brenna dragged him up to her chambers.

Their chambers.

That thought was unfathomable to him.

To have left his onerous clan, lied his way into this one, found a love he'd not believed possible, and become part of this new clan. 'Twas like something of a fairy folk tale.

"Are ye certain 'tis what ye want, Brenna?" Rafe tugged at her hand as she rushed through the door. "I mean, with all ye've been through, and my MacKay clan . . ."

Brenna pulled him into the room with her.

"Weel, 'tis a bit late to change my mind now. The priest did say 'man and wife.'"

Rafe flicked his eyes to the bed. "Nay, ye can still change your mind. 'Tisn't official, yet."

She twirled into his arms, her face a bright, smiling light shining up at him.

"No' yet. Then we should make it so."

He peered at her with a forceful gaze before inclining his head to catch her lips in a simple, delicate kiss. Brenna responded, her lips searching his, and he became more aggressive. Her kiss was so galvanizing, a tremor of excited expectation coursed through him. Those same sensations must have rocked Brenna, as her hips moved against his, inviting more. He groaned and rose to that invitation.

Brenna twirled again, leaving his embrace to move toward the hearth. Keeping one coy eye on Rafe, she slipped the neckline of her creamy gown over one slender shoulder, letting it fall so the curve of her breast peeked above the wide neckline. Rafe was rooted in his spot by the door, unable to drag his burning gaze from what she offered. His blood pounded in his head, echoed in his ears, and throbbed in his cock.

She tugged at the laced neckline so the other shoulder fell. Her perfectly formed breasts sprung out of her wedding gown, soft, pink-tipped ripe fruit, and the vision of her broke him. Tearing his own tunic over his head, he reached for her, his bronzed chest pressing against those supple breasts. He reclaimed her mouth with savage intensity, a sense of ownership, of knowing that this woman was now his and his alone. Rafe couldn't contain himself any longer.

He walked her backwards to the bedding. Brenna's hands worked her dress off her legs as they moved. Rafe lay her on the bed with surprising gentleness of all the passion that burned from him. In a breathless movement, he dropped his kilt to the floor, and stood for a moment, allowing her to study his body.

And study it she did. Brenna's eyes roved from his riotous raven-locks to his smoldering eyes, over his sculpted chest and belly to his turgid sword that sprung from his eager loins. His thick legs, like tree trunks, only showcased his power even more. The man was a warrior in the truest sense of the word. And he belonged to her.

Then he lowered his body onto hers, tracing the lines of her curves with a light finger – over her breasts, her pale belly, her firm hips – and his touches were so arousing that tremors of excitement streamed through her. Then his mouth followed the path of his fingers, and her tremors became outright quivering.

"Please," she begged of her new husband.

Rafe's eyes squinted, teasing her desire until it was unbearable.

Then, as his lips found hers, so did his manhood find her ready opening. And when he took her, his cock was hot and commanding, and she lost herself in the sensations that he wrought inside her.

They rode together, moving and shifting like the tides, and when he cried out his climax, he wrapped his arms around her, enclosing her within his giant warmth, and they became one.

Their fall back to earth was slow and cloying, and the chill in the air cooled their skin, making Brenna shiver. Rafe tucked the tartan coverlet around them, sharing his own heat. Sleep overwhelmed them, limbs entwined. And when Rafe rolled to the side in his sleep, Brenna slipped a slender arm over his waist and relaxed against his back to keep that touching bond even as they slept.

To Rafe, with Brenna curled around his back, he was aware that she was protecting him, his own tiny warrior who didn't let him go, even when life was at its worst.

Rafe was now a Fraser. The clan-less warrior had found a lost warrior lass, and together they found a home.

The End

If you love this book, be sure to leave a review! Reviews are life blood for authors, and I appreciate every review I receive!

Want more from Michelle? Click below to receive Gavin, the free Glen Highland Romance short ebook, free books, updates, and more in your inbox

https://linktr.ee/mddalrympleauthor

Love Highlanders? Try Michelle's Ancient Celtic Highlander series!
The Maiden of the Storm

An excerpt from the Celtic Highland Maidens series —

This new series will take us back in time, to a place where the Ancient Celts, the Caledonii tribe, fought for their land and their people against the Romans in 209 AD.

The Maiden of the Storm

Northern Scotland, north of Antoine's Wall, Caledonii Tribe, 209 AD

Rumors circulated of Roman Centauriae extending their patrols north beyond Antoine's wall, what they referred to disdainfully as cnap-starra. And her father's tribe watched from their secluded positions as those soldiers behaved in stupid, overly confident ways. If they wouldn't have risked giving away their positions, the painted men might have laughed at the ill-mannered soldiering of these weighted-down Romans.

Ru was chieftain of his tribe, a remote relative of the great King Gartnaith Blogh who himself managed to run the Roman fools from the Caledonii Highlands. 'Twas said the king laughed with zeal as the Latin devils, in their flaying and rusted Roman armor, scrambled over the low stone wall. As though a minor cnap-starra could stop the mighty Caledonii warriors from striking fear into the heart of their Centauriae. Fools.

But speculation blossomed of rogue Roman soldiers venturing far north of the wall, a reckless endeavor if Ru's daughter, Riana, ever heard one. Warriors from her father's tribe and other nearby tribes traveled across the mountainous countryside, through the wide glen to meet them.

Thus far, the soldiers had remained close to the wall, fearing to leave the false security it provided. Ru's warriors had struck down one or two that meandered away from that security, wounding them, perchance fatally, with a well-aimed throw of a spear. The diminutive Roman soldiers, even clad in their hopeful leather and metal armor, were no match for the powerful throw of a Caledonii spear.

This most recent Roman soldier, however, appeared less resilient, less aggressive than his previous counterparts. Though clad in full Roman military garb, he wasn't paying attention to his surroundings — distracted as he was. The Centauriae had traversed the low mountains and lochs to their hidden land. And he was alone. Ru noted his lean-muscled build and made an abrupt decision.

"Dinna kill this lad," he whispered to Dunbraith, his military adviser and old friend. "We should keep him, enslave him. Melt his iron and armor into weapons. And use his knowledge against these pissants. Give them a bit of their own medicine."

Dunbraith's face, blue woad paint lines mixed with blood red, was fearsome and thoughtful. "Severus is defeated," his growling voice responded. "The Roman lines are scattered. 'Tis a safe assumption they will not even try to retrieve the lad."

A frightening smile crossed his face, one that Ru knew well. A cruel smile that didn't reach his eyes.

Ru nodded his agreement and waved his hand at his Imannae, a young Caledonii eager to prove his worth. The young man positioned himself just beyond the leaves of the scrub bush in which he hid, narrowed his eyes at his prey, and launched a strong-armed throw of his sharpened spear.

The Imannae's throw was perfect, catching the young Roman's upper arm in a sharp drive. The lad cried out and dropped to his knees in pain and shock. Ru and his warriors moved in as silent as nightfall.

The Maiden of the Storm

An Excerpt from An Echo in the Glen – Book 7

It's here! Gavin's Story!

Jenny pursed her lips and blew her light blonde hair away from her face, then closed the door. Her hands were full with a tray of uneaten food and damp clothes. Just as the latch sealed the door, the platter was lifted from her juggling hands.

Her eyes flew to the man towering over her, a sandy-haired giant clad in a tunic stained from the day's work and a pair of loose braies tucked into muddy boots. The man held the tray aloft as Jenny righted herself.

Gavin's eyes alighted at Jenny, her way of knowing he was delighted to see her, and his peek-a-boo dimples cut endearing dots into his cheeks. The dimples were not the result of a happy smile; rather they appeared whenever Gavin pursed his lips as well, oft making the fierce MacLeod giant look like an over-sized laddie.

And his pursed lips were not without merit. Jenny was torn between lifting her hands to cup one dimpled cheek and gripping her own middy kirtle in distress. Her hands now empty, she did both.

His hazel brown eyes burned through her, his own distress evident on his face. Most likely, he'd just left Ewan's side, trying to keep his best friend and MacLeod Laird busy while his dainty wife convalesced.

"How is she?" Gavin asked in a tight voice.

Meg and Ewan's first babe had been successfully delivered from Meg mere days after Candlemas, and in Elspeth's estimation, the birth had been uneventful, even gone well. Birth was an anxious prospect, Elspeth had told Jenny only a fortnight before the birth, because of Meg's tiny frame and narrow hips. The lass had bore down, drew from an inner well of will and strength, and a screaming, black-haired Caitir was born in the early hours of the morn amid the newly blessed incandescent light.

Then Father MacBain had baptized the lassie in the main hall of the keep and a joyous celebration was had by all. Meg appeared to be in high spirits, even shoving Jenny from the room so she and Ewan might care for the wee bairn alone.

'Twas a memorable night for Jenny, for two reasons. 'Twas the night Gavin offered for her hand, convinced, finally, of the joys to be found in the bounds of marriage and children, of the exultation of a meeting of hearts and desire.

Unfortunately, on the heels of such bliss came a harrowing disaster. Meg fell ill.

Look for the pre-order link for An Echo in the Glen, coming soon!

A Note on History —

For this story, I took the man who left the MacKay's in my previous book, The Seduction of the Glen, and gave him his story. So often, our villains are just ordinary people who find themselves on the wrong path. They become villains when they like to too much and remain there. Rafe MacKay wanted to change his circumstances – he didn't want to stay on that path – and his story needed to be told. In this book, Robert the Bruce and the Scots War of Independence really takes a back seat to the idea of "while the cat's away, the mice will play" idea.

However, some historical elements I tried to keep as aligned as possible, such as Robert the Bruce moving around the lowlands as his army advanced and the clansmen flocking to his banner when they could. And while the Scots War of Independence did much to unite the clans in a large sense, many clans still had feuds and skirmishes. Unity, as we well know, is not always perfect. The idea of one clan taking advantage of the "cat" being away, as we saw in *Seduction*, was continued here.

Once again, I hope the history seems as real for you as it does for me. And if there are any mistakes in the history, those are completely mine – reconstructed for creative licensing, of course!

And I have a personal history with someone who suffered from dementia. This book is dedicated to my grandfather.

A Thank You–

Thank you to the most amazing readers on the planet. That you keep coming back – that you want to read more, is what keeps me going. Thank you for your feedback, commentary, reviews, and cheers! Also, thank you for reading book after book. It only makes me want to write more.

I also need to thank my beta readers and those who help with editing and refining – Sophie in particular – you all make such a great team for me, help me edit and finish crafting a great story. I cannot thank you enough!

A special thank you to the real-world Dawn Fraser, who reads all my stuff, gives me feedback when she thinks it's warranted, and asked when she would get to be in a book. Thank you, Dawnie, for giving me another real-world aspect to pull from for this book! And for being there for me each and every time I needed you!

And a final thanks to my family – my kids and hubby – who are ever so forgiving to mommy when she has writing on deck and needs to lock herself away!

About the Author

Michelle Deerwester-Dalrymple is a professor of writing and an author. She started reading when she was 3 years old, writing when she was 4, and published her first poem at age 16. She has written articles and essays on a variety of topics, including several texts on writing for middle and high school students. She is also working on a novel inspired by actual events. She lives in California with her family of seven.

You can visit her web page, sign up for her newsletter, and follow all her socials at:

https://linktr.ee/mddalrympleauthor

Also by the Author:

Glen Highland Romance

To Dance in the Glen – Book 1
The Lady of the Glen – Book 2
The Exile of the Glen – Book 3
The Jewel of the Glen – Book 4
The Seduction of the Glen – Book 5
The Warrior of the Glen – Book 6
An Echo in the Glen – Book 7 coming soon!
The Blackguard of the Glen – Book 8 coming soon!

The Celtic Highland Maidens
The Maiden of the Storm
The Maiden of the Grove
The Maiden of the Celts – Coming soon!
The Maiden of the Loch – coming soon!

As M.D. Dalrymple - Men in Uniform

Night Shift – Book 1
Day Shift – Book 2
Overtime – Book 3
Holiday Pay – Book 4
School Resource Officer – book 5
Holdover – book 6 coming soon!

The Warrior of the Glen